David Almond

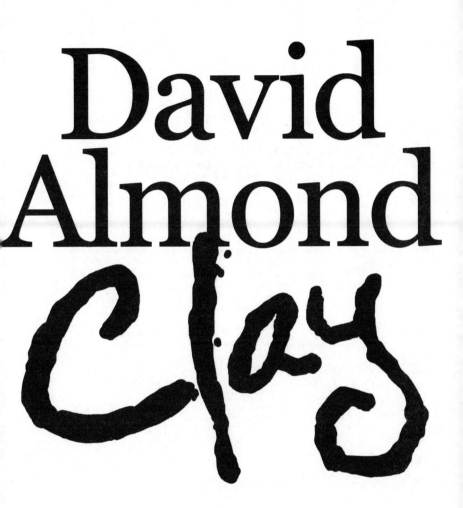

Clay

Hodder
Children's
Books

a division of Hodder Headline Limited

For Sara Jane
who works wonders with clay

One

One

He arrived in Felling on a bright and icy February morning. Not so long ago, but it was a different age. I was with Geordie Craggs, like I always was back then. We were swaggering along like always, laughing and joking like always. We passed a Players back and forward and blew long strings of smoke into the air. We'd just been on the altar. We were heading for Braddock's Garden. We were on Watermill Lane when a red taxi rattled past us. Black fumes belched from it. The sign at the top said it was from down at the coast.

'What's that doing up here?' said Geordie.

A bit of communion wafer was still stuck to my teeth. I poked it free with my tongue and swallowed it, then drew on the cigarette again.

'God knows,' I said.

The taxi stopped fifty yards away, outside Crazy Mary's house. Crazy came lolloping out with her red hair flying. She had a big flappy flowery dress and tartan slippers on. The kid got out of the taxi. He pulled a battered brown suitcase after him. Crazy paid the driver then the two of them headed for her front door. She looked back at us. She tried to put her arm around the kid but he twisted away and went inside. Crazy followed him and the door slammed shut.

The taxi driver leaned out of his window as he went past.

'What you two nebbing at?' he said.

'Nowt much,' I said.

'Why don't you nick off back to Whitley Bay?' said Geordie.

'Aye,' I said. 'Nick off, Fishface.'

And we laughed and belted on towards the garden yelling,

'Fishface! Fishface! Fishface!'

We went through the ancient iron gate, ducked through the thorns, splashed through the edge of the clay pond, went into the quarry, went into the cave. There was writing on the wall again. We held matches up to it. All it said was, *We're watching you. Your doomd.* Then a big black *X*. Somebody had tried to draw a skull as well but it looked like they'd given up cos they were too useless.

'Thick as clarts,' I said.

I wiped dirt over it all.

Geordie lit another fag. He sharpened his knife on a stone.

He pointed it at me.

'Soon there'll be a proper battle,' he said.

I sucked the fag.

'Aye,' I said.

'It'll be just them and us,' he said.

I shivered. I tried to laugh.

'The Battle of Braddock's Garden,' I said.

I looked out at the sheer craggy quarry walls, the thick weeds, the deep clay pond, the ruins of Braddock's house above. The sparrowhawk flew out from its stony nest and flapped up into the open sky.

'Who was that at Crazy's?' I said.

He shrugged.

'God knows,' he said. 'Wouldn't like to be him, though, holed up with that loony.'

He took a syrup of figs bottle out of his pocket and lobbed it over. It was half-full of the wine that he'd stolen after Mass that morning. I screwed the top off and swigged and smacked me lips. The wine was sticky and sweet and you could soon feel the little bit of dreaminess it brought.

'Pinching altar wine's a sin,' I said.

We laughed and snapped some sticks, getting a fire ready.

I pointed to the ground.

'You'll burn in Hell, George Craggs,' I said.

'Naa,' said Geordie. 'Not for that. You go to Hell for proper sins. Like nicking a million quid.'

'Or killing somebody,' I said.

'Aye.' He stabbed the knife into the ground. 'Murder!' He swigged the wine and swiped his hand across his lips. 'I dreamed I killed Mouldy the other night.'

'Did you?'

'Aye.'

'Was there loads of blood?'

'Gallons. Blood and guts everywhere.'

'Great!'

'I did it here. I stabbed him in the heart then I chopped his head off and I hoyed it in the pond.'

We giggled.

'Probly that'd not be a sin at all,' I said. 'Probly you'd go straight to Heaven for getting rid of a thing like Mouldy.'

'Course you would,' said Geordie. 'The whole world'd be better off without things like Mouldy.'

'Aye.'

We were quiet while we thought of Mouldy. We listened to the noises in the quarry.

'You seen how big he's getting?' I said.

'Aye.'

'Bliddy Hell,' I whispered.

'Aye. Bliddy Hell. He's turning to a monster.'

Two

There was no mystery. It turned out the kid was called Stephen Rose. He was from Whitley Bay. He was just a bit older than us. The story was he'd gone away to Bennett College to train to be a priest. He went when he was eleven, which wasn't strange back then in the 1960s. We knew loads of lads that did it. Like many of them, though, Stephen couldn't stand it and he came back out again two or three years later. He'd just been home a month when his dad dropped dead with a stroke. Then his mother went mad and was taken away in the middle of a stormy night to Prudhoe. Stephen was all alone. The Poor Clares were going to take him in, then somehow they found out there was a distant aunt, Crazy Mary, up here in Felling, and so he came to her. The plan was that his mother'd be out soon, they'd set up home down at the coast again, everything would settle down again. But when I heard my parents on about it, it seemed there wouldn't be much chance of that. They'd heard she was truly barmy. She'd gone way way round the bend.

'Worse than Crazy Mary?' I said.

Mam glared at me.

'Don't call the poor woman that,' she said. 'She's just a devout and troubled soul.'

'Sorry,' I said.

'You don't know how lucky you are,' she said. 'There but for the grace of God . . .'

'What?' I groaned. 'You worried about me sanity, Mother?'

I twisted my mouth and stuck my tongue out and drooled.

'Stop it!' she snapped. 'Don't tempt fate.'

She crossed herself.

'Maybe we should call her Holy Mary,' she said. 'Have you seen anybody else so devout, anybody else that prays so hard, anybody else so filled with yearning?'

I shook my head.

'Well, then,' she said. 'Did you know there's stories that there's saints in Mary's past?'

'Saints?'

'Way back in her family. Back in Ireland, where the Doonans came from long ago.'

Dad laughed.

'In the olden days,' he said, 'when saints walked in every village and an angel sat in every tree.'

At first we hardly saw Stephen Rose. He didn't turn up at school like we'd expected him to. Mam said he must still be grieving, poor bairn. Dad said aye, he'd been through too much for a young'n. Geordie reckoned there was something dead weird about him. Geordie knew somebody that lived just down the street from Crazy. They'd seen Stephen in the garden at night, staring up at the moon.

'At the moon?' I said.

'Aye.' He grinned. 'Like he was moonbathing, like he'd mixed the sun up with the moon. Have you seen his skin?'

'What d'you mean?'

'It's like wax, man. And have you smelled him?'

'How would I smell him?'

'I have. I passed him in the street. He was out walking with Mary, a pair of loonies. You know what she smells like.'

'Aye.' Old, even though Mam said she was no age at all, and kind of sickly and sweet.

'He's worse, man. Yuk. Just imagine being in there with the pair of them.'

We were walking home from school, passing close by Crazy's house. We looked at the windows, the ancient net curtains there, the silhouette of the Sacred Heart medallion there like in all the Catholic houses. There was white smoke drifting up from the chimney.

'And he does other stuff in the garden and all,' said Geordie.

'Stuff?'

'So they say. Some days he's out there in Crazy's shed for hours at a time. There's banging and thumping and whimpering and howling.'

'Howling?'

'Aye, so they say. Oh, my God! It's Mouldy!'

We stopped quickly. We squeezed into a privet hedge. My heart was thumping. I could hardly breathe.

'We're safe,' said Geordie. 'He's going the other way.'

I peeped out from the hedge. There he was, Martin Mould, Mouldy, heading down to Heworth. Even from this distance you could see how big he'd got. He seemed bigger every time we saw him. He was already loads bigger than when there'd been the last battle. He and his mates had ambushed us outside the graveyard that day. I remembered Mouldy's massive hands around my throat. I remembered the thump of his winkle-picker boots across my cheek. I remembered his evil eyes, his fierce breath, his vicious spit. Sometimes I woke up in the night from dreams of it all happening again.

I waited with Geordie in the hedge and watched and

trembled. Mouldy went into The Swan. He was only sixteen but already he drank like a man.

'We got to get more kids,' said Geordie.

'Aye,' I said.

We moved on. I tried to shift my mind from thoughts of Mouldy.

'Howling?' I said.

'Aye. That's the story. Howling. Yowling fit to wake the dead.'

Three

The next Saturday was a good one. There were two funerals, one at nine o'clock, one at ten. I served at both of them with Geordie.

The first was for a bloke from Stoneygate. He'd fallen out of a bus on Sunderland Road. He was ancient, so there wasn't that much weeping and wailing. We did the usual stuff in church then we got into the black car that followed the hearse down to the graveyard at Heworth. We swung the incense there and splashed the holy water and Father O'Mahoney said the words about being dust and unto dust we shall return. Sometimes one of the family came straight out with a tip when it was all over, but sometimes you had to drop a hint or two. This time the likely-looking one was a bloke in a natty blue suit. He was the old bloke's son. He'd come up specially from London. I caught up with him as the mourners headed back to the black cars.

'Sorry for your loss,' I said quietly.

'Thank you,' he said.

'Me name's David,' I said.

'Thank you, David.'

'And that's me friend, George. We were happy to serve this morning.'

The woman he was with nudged him and whispered to him.

'Thank you,' he said again.

He shoved a folded note into my hand.

I grinned when we were back in the car. I put my hand on Geordie's knee and opened it and showed the note.

'Ten bob!' he said.

Father O'Mahoney coughed. He was in the front with the undertaker and watching us through the driver's mirror.

'Now, then, boys,' he said. 'A bit of respect, eh?'

'Sorry, Father,' we said together.

'Ten bob!' we whispered and I saw the priest look down and smile.

The next one wasn't so easy. It was another bloke, but younger this time and with a son and a daughter just a bit older than us. Even Father O'Mahoney had a tear in his eye and he had to keep blowing his nose in a big blue handkerchief. The bloke's wife broke down at the graveyard and yelled, 'Why? Why? Why?'

Geordie and I had seen it all before so we knew to just ignore it and go through the motions. Funnily enough it was at funerals like those that the tips came easiest. A bloke in a black trilby came over and gave us a half-crown each and told us we were good lads.

'Life's the thing, boys,' he said. 'You understand that?'

'Yes,' I said.

'Be sure you make the most of it, now. Afore you know it, you'll be . . .'

'We will, Mister,' said Geordie.

'Good lads.'

'Five more bob!' we whispered.

Then I saw Stephen Rose. He was standing among the graves. Like Geordie said his face was like wax. We passed really close to him. He had a slab of yellowy clay under his arm.

'Are you all right, Stephen?' said Father O'Mahoney.

It was like he didn't hear at first, then he blinked and said,

'Aye, Father.'

'And where's your aunt today?'

'Don't know, Father. In the house, Father.'

'Tell her I was asking. I'll make another visit in a day or two.'

'Aye, Father.'

The priest walked on, then he paused again.

'This is two good lads I've got with me,' he said. 'Maybe they could make pals of yours.'

'Aye, Father.'

'That's grand, then.'

Stephen moved closer to me. I understood what Geordie had said about the smell of him.

'The grave diggers gave me this,' he said. 'It come from deep deep down.'

He ran his hand over the clay. He licked his fingers and pressed them into it. He picked a stone or something out of it and inspected it.

'A bit of bone,' he said.

He quickly pressed three holes and a slit: two eyes, a nose, a mouth. He held it up and rocked it in the air like it was a puppet. He made it talk in a squeaky voice.

'Hello,' it said. 'What's your name?'

'Davie,' I said.

'Davie, man!' called Geordie from the door of the car.

'It's hopeless clay,' said Stephen. He scratched with his fingernail and showed how it just crumbled away. 'See?' he said.

'Aye.'

He waved his hand across my eyes then he stared at me and grinned.

'You didn't say hello to it,' he said. 'Go on, say hello to it.'

I turned to Geordie.

'Go on,' said Stephen. 'It's just a joke.'

'Hello,' I murmured.

'Hello, Davie,' squeaked the clay. 'Thank you for believing in me.'

I shook my head and rolled my eyes, like I'd fallen for a trick. I grinned back at Stephen.

'I'm Stephen Rose, Davie,' he said.

'Davie!' yelled Geordie.

I ran to the car. We headed out of the graveyard. The priest watched me through the mirror.

'Are you all right, Davie?' he said.

'Aye, Father.'

'That's grand,' he said. 'You could be just what that lad needs.'

Then he smiled.

'A profitable morning, then?' he said.

'Aye, Father,' we answered.

Four

'They're crackers,' said Geordie.

'What?' I said.

'Wacko. The whole damn lot of them. Always have been. Always will be. So me dad says.'

'Aye?' I said.

'Aye. And Stephen's granda was the biggest nutter of the lot.'

'How does your dad know?'

'He used to see him, man. They called him Rocky Rose. He did hypnotism tricks in the bars in Cullercoats and Whitley Bay. Got people to drop their trousers and wet their pants and that . . .'

'He didn't.'

'He did, man. He used to do tricks and get paid in pints. He did it on the beach and all. Me dad says he seen him when he was a bairn. Said he seen one old biddy dive in the sea with all her clothes on. And there was a bloke flapping his arms and screaming cos he thought he was a seagull.'

'Bliddy Hell.'

'Aye. Bliddy Hell. That's the lot that he comes from. One part of the family ran a freak stall at the fairs. There were derelicts and down-and-outs and dreamers. It seems Rocky ended up living in a tent in Plessey Woods, all horrible and hairy and running away if anybody come near.'

'Bliddy Hell.'

'Aye. I know. He's dead now, and the freak stall's gone. But no wonder Stephen's a bit . . .'

'Aye. Just imagine.'

We tried to imagine, then Geordie said,

'The story is that Stephen's mam and dad were trying to get a bit more civilised, living in a proper house like proper people do and having proper jobs and that, but . . .'

'They couldn't do it.'

'No.'

'Just imagine. If there's all that in your family . . .'

'Like your granda . . .'

'And your mother . . .'

'And your only bloody aunty . . .'

We lurched about a bit and grunted like we'd both gone daft. Then we burst out laughing.

'Bliddy Hell,' I said. 'He's doomed! Doomed!'

We were at the cave. We both had knives. We were sharpening sticks. We were going to set them up at the quarry entrance, stick them in the mud, pointing upwards, like a trap.

'Me dad says he just needs some mates,' I said.

'Does he?'

'Aye. And me mother.'

I whipped the knife across the stick. I pressed the point to my palm. Needle-sharp. I imagined Mouldy stepping on it. I imagined it going straight through the sole to his foot. I thought of blood poisoning, thought of Mouldy up in the Queen Elizabeth Hospital, and the doctor saying to Mouldy's mother, 'There's no way we can save it, Mrs Mould. The foot has to come off.' I thought of Mouldy hobbling around Pelaw for the rest of his life. I bent the point over, blunted it, but I didn't let Geordie see.

'She said we should call on him,' I said.

'She's joking.'

'She said put yourself in his shoes.'

'What did you say?'

'I said nowt. I said we would if we had the time. She said we had all the time in the world.'

'Huh.'

Geordie picked another stick up.

'We should set up nooses and all,' he said. 'Hang them down from them hawthorns so they run straight into them and get strangled. And we should definitely set tripwires to send them into the pond.'

We had a laugh, thinking about them hanging in the trees and flopping in the pond.

Then I leaned back on the stone. It was all stupid. Mouldy was the only really evil one. His mates were ordinary kids just like us. They were playing, just like us, they were scared and excited, just like us. The only reason we battled with them was because they came from Pelaw and we came from Felling. We pretended we hated them because they were Proddies and they pretended they hated us because we were Catholics but that was really nothing to do with it. It was just the Felling/Pelaw thing. It had gone on for ever, even in my dad's day. He used to laugh when he heard about it, still going on, and when my mam tried to get worried he told her it was nowt, it was just a game. But Mouldy. He was different. When he had his hands around my throat that day, his own mates had to help Geordie to pull him off. When he kicked me in the face he hadn't held back. When he snarled in my face it seemed full of real hatred, real evil. 'Catholic bastard,' he'd snarled. 'Felling Catholic bastard.' And I'd carried the bruises and the fright for days.

'Do you think he's scary?' said Geordie.

'Mouldy?'

'Of course Mouldy's scary. But I mean Stephen Rose. Do you think *he's* scary?'

'Dunno. He's just a kid, just like us.'

'Just like us? Bliddy Hell, man. Howling in the shed, carrying lumps of muck in the bloody graveyard . . .'

'Clay.'

'Whatever. Living with Crazy Mary. Mother crackers, father dead, grandad wild.'

'Suppose he might be scary if you put it like that.'

'Might be? He might be bliddy terrifying, man.'

He laughed.

'Are you thinking what I'm thinking?' he said.

'Dunno,' I said.

'Well you should be,' he said. 'A lad like Stephen Rose might be just what we need.'

He stabbed his stick hard into the ground.

'Howay,' he said. 'Let's go and rattle Crazy's door.'

Five

Crazy's door was green and the paint was peeling off. The knocker was rusty and it squealed when Geordie lifted it. He had to shove it down to make it knock. There was no answer. I breathed a sigh of relief and turned around to leave.

'Howay,' I said. 'They must be out.'

But Geordie knocked again, and then again.

'Geordie, man,' I said.

Then there were footsteps at the other side of the door and Crazy peeped out through the skinny letter box.

'Who's there?' she said.

'We've come to see Stephen Rose,' said Geordie.

He leaned close to the door. He pulled me close as well.

'Look,' he said. 'It's just us, Missus . . .'

'Miss Doonan,' I whispered to him.

'Just us, Miss Doonan. You've seen us on the altar. We thought Stephen might want to come out for a bit.'

Her eyes rolled. She blinked. The door creaked open a few inches and her waxy face appeared.

'On the altar?' she said.

'Aye,' I said.

'So you're good boys?' she said.

'Aye,' said Geordie.

'You know our mams and dads, Miss Doonan,' I said.

Her eyes were still for a moment while she regarded me.

'I can see your mother's face in you,' she said to me.

She opened the door a bit wider and stuck her skinny arm out. She pulled back the flowery sleeve with her other hand and pointed to a place under the elbow.

'Your mother touched me there once,' she said. 'She said, "There now, Mary. There now. Don't trouble yourself." I can feel her fingers now.'

She stroked her skin at the memory.

'Is he in?' said Geordie.

She narrowed her eyes. She stared past us into the empty sky. She said, 'And I can hear her voice. "There now, Mary." She said that. Like a mother would.'

She reached out and touched my cheek and I flinched.

'Did you know that a boy has been sent to me?' she said.

'Aye,' said Geordie. 'We've come to see him, Missus.'

'To see him?'

'Aye, Missus.'

She crossed herself.

'You have been drawn to this place,' she said.

'We could be his mates,' said Geordie.

She opened the door wider.

'Mebbe he has need of you,' she said.

Geordie nudged me with his elbow and stepped inside.

'There's holy water there,' she said. 'Cross yourselves and come inside.'

We dipped our fingers into the bowl on the table inside the door. She watched us make the sign of the cross on ourselves. We rolled our eyes at each other and followed her through the narrow hall. There were dusty plaster angels flying on the wall. There was a great big ancient picture of Jesus with the crown of thorns stabbing his skull and his chest opened up to show his massive sacred heart. There was the scent of piss and the air was cold and the floor was just bare boards.

'He was to have been a priest,' she said.

'We know,' I said.

'Right from the very start he had a holy heart,' she said.

Geordie trembled as he held his laughter in.

'This is me great great great aunt Annie,' she said.

She pointed to the wall, to an ancient photo of a tiny blurry woman smoking a pipe and standing outside a tiny filthy cottage.

'That's Connemara,' she said. 'Annie spent every day of her life on that blessed bog.'

'Aye?' snorted Geordie.

'Aye.' She turned her eyes towards the ceiling. 'And she's in Heaven now if anybody is.'

In the kitchen there was a battered aluminium teapot and two mugs on a table. There was bread and a lump of margarine and a pot of jam with a knife stuck in. A prayer book was open. A statue of Our Lady was silhouetted against the back window. Outside in the little garden the grass and weeds were knee-high, with a channel worn through towards the door of the black shed out there.

'Is he in?' I said.

'No,' she said. 'He's out. He's at his sacred work.'

She opened the door. A huge crow croaked then flapped away into another garden. There a baby crying its eyes out somewhere.

'Wait here,' she said.

She went to the shed. Geordie and me snorted.

'Bliddy Hell,' I said. 'Let's get out before we're trapped.'

We snorted again.

She opened the shed door. A shaft of sunlight was shining down inside. We saw Stephen in there, turning to Crazy Mary, then peering out at us. Then Crazy came back out. She raised her hands towards us.

'Aye!' she called. 'Aye! He says come to him!'

We didn't move.

'Come!' she called.

'Hell's teeth,' I whispered.

'Howay, man,' said Geordie.

Six

He was sitting at a bench with a knife in his hand. He was carving a piece of wood, a snapped branch. It had an arm, a leg, the start of a face. There were shavings on his arms and on the bench and floor. Dust poured through the shaft of light that fell through a little window in the pitched roof. The corners of the shed were deep in shadow.

'I'm doing this for the priest,' he said.

'Father O'Mahoney,' I said.

'Aye. Him. He says the devil makes work for idle hands so I got to keep busy. Look,' he said, and he pointed to another bench. There were more figures on it, carved out of curved and twisted wood so they seemed to be staggering or leaning or stunted. 'They're no good,' he said. 'And neither's that.' He pointed at a crude clay figure. Its body was crumbling away. An arm and a leg had fallen off. He poked it and another leg fell off.

'See?' he said. 'Clay's the stuff I need. But there's nowt decent here.'

He reached out and quickly touched my cheek. I flinched.

'This is what clay should turn out like,' he said. 'Like living flesh. Like a living body. But look.'

He punched the figure and it burst into fragments and dust.

'See?' he said.

He lifted one of the wooden figures and snapped it fast and easy between his hands.

'See?' he said.

He turned and stared at Crazy.

'See?' he said to her. 'I telt you, Aunty Mary. There's nowt that's any good.'

She walked back to the house and watched us through the kitchen window. He kicked the shed door shut.

'She's crackers,' he said. 'They're the apostles. He wants them for the school or something. They're crap.'

He stabbed the knife into the bench. He blew up into the falling dust and it danced and sparkled in the shaft of light all around him.

'That's what we're made of,' he said. 'Dust. That's why clay's best. Wood's been alive already so it's dead.

And how can you get something that's dead turn to something that's alive again?'

'Dunno,' I said.

'You can't. You got to start from the start again, from something that's never been nowt.'

Geordie and me looked at each other.

'Like God did,' said Stephen.

He watched me. I tried to flick away the dust he'd left on my cheek.

'You got a match?' said Stephen.

Geordie took a box out of his pocket and rattled it. Stephen took it. He kicked the door open again. He got a handful of shavings and put them on the ground outside. He struck a match and lit the shavings and put the apostles on top. Me and Geordie stayed close together and we watched the fire burn. Stephen crouched down beside it and warmed his hands at the flames.

'See,' he said. 'You do it just like that.'

'Bliddy Hell,' murmured Geordie.

'Fire hardens clay,' said Stephen. 'But wood . . . huh!'

Crazy watched us and chewed her nails.

Stephen shadowed his face from the sun with his hand. He peered at us.

'What you after, anyway?' he said.

I shook my head.

'Nowt,' I said.

He grinned at me.

'Well, that's easy enough,' he said. He pretended to throw something gently to me. 'Here, have some nowt.'

The apostles spat and hissed and twisted as they burned below us.

'We know where there's some clay for you,' said Geordie. 'Loads of it.'

'Is that right?' said Stephen.

'Aye,' I said.

'We can take you to it,' said Geordie.

'Take me, then,' said Stephen.

He smiled at me.

'Take me,' he said. 'I'll come with you.'

So we walked away from the blazing apostles and back into Crazy Mary's house. Crazy dithered around Stephen in the kitchen. She tried to put her arm around him, but he just told her, 'Let me be. I've got things to do with me friends.'

We went back through the hallway. I dipped my hand into the holy water and crossed myself again. Then we took Stephen out on to Watermill Lane and down to Braddock's Garden and we led him to the clay pond where he pushed the spawn aside and reached down deep into the milky water and lifted out a dripping handful of pale clay.

'Brilliant!' he breathed.

He stood up and held it towards my face. It oozed and splashed down on to the ground between us.

'This is it,' he said. 'This is the real stuff.'

He moved close to me.

'Say hello to it,' he said. He laughed. 'Just think what we could make with this.'

Seven

Saturday evening, the same week. I went to St Patrick's. I knelt in the dark confessional. I could see Father O'Mahoney's face through the grille. I wondered if I should try to disguise my voice, but I knew, like always, it would be no good. Of course he'd know who I was. And did it matter? There was nothing unusual about me. There was nothing unusual about my sins. Back in those days, the things I did wrong were tiny, insignificant. It was like I was just making stuff up.

I started with the words I'd been taught when I was a little kid.

'Bless me, Father, for I have sinned. It is two weeks since my last confession.'

'Yes, my son?' he said.

He sighed and waited.

It was always best to get the worst out first.

'I drank some altar wine, Father.'

'Did you now? This is both theft and blasphemy.'

'Yes, Father. I understand. Sorry, Father.'

'It is not to me that you must apologise in here.'

'No, Father.'

'And will you do it again?'

'No, Father. And I stole some cigarettes from my dad.'

'And smoked them?'

'Yes, Father. And the cigarettes of somebody else's dad. And I have coveted other people's goods. Their money, Father. And I have called people cruel names. And—'

'Have you now? What kind of names?'

'Fishface, Father.'

'Fishface?'

I heard his little snort of laughter.

'Yes, Father.'

'That is terrible. What else?'

'I have laughed at people who are in distress.'

'Which is a lack of charity and which will cause pain.'

'Yes, Father. It will.'

'And will you change your ways, my son?'

'Yes, Father.'

'Anything else now?'

I gritted my teeth. I thought of Geordie's older sister,

Noreen. She was sixteen, in the sixth form. She was gorgeous. He waited. He sighed.

'Anything else now?' he repeated. 'Remember that God sees everything.'

'I have had impure thoughts, Father.'

'Have you now?'

'Yes, Father.'

'And did you act on these thoughts?'

'What, Father? Oh, no, Father.'

'That's grand. Anything else now?'

'No, Father.'

'And do you feel sorrow for your sins?'

I paused and pondered. I thought for an instant of the bitter, beguiling taste of the cigarettes. I thought of Noreen lying in Geordie's back garden last summer.

'Do you?' said the priest again.

'Yes, Father. Definitely, Father.'

I saw his hand moving across his face as he absolved me.

'Your sins are forgiven,' he said. 'Say five Hail Marys and one Our Father and resolve that you will be good.'

'Yes, Father. I will, Father.'

'And keep away from the altar wine.'

'Yes, Father.'

'And your dad's cigarettes.'

'Yes, Father.'

'Now go in peace to love and serve the Lord.'

I stepped back out of the confessional into the half-lit church. I knelt at the altar rail and said my penance. The murmur of the next penitent echoed gently around the walls.

'And deliver us from evil,' I said at last and I hurried out into the evening. I felt as light as air. Geordie was already done. He was waiting outside. He sparked up a couple of Players and we breathed long plumes of smoke into the air.

'It's great feeling holy, isn't it?' he said.

'Aye,' I said. I held up my hands to the sky. 'Glory be!'

We laughed and walked fast and kept knocking into each other and started wrestling in the street with our fags stuck in our mouths. Some bloke came out of the Half Way House and nearly walked straight into us.

'Daft kids,' he said. 'What do you think you're doing?'

'Bugger off,' said Geordie.

'Aye,' I said. 'Bugger off, Fishface.'

And we ran and he chased us but he couldn't keep up. We ran across the square then we stopped and I yelled and yelled.

'Fishface! Fishface! Ahahahahaha!'

I clapped my hand across my mouth.

'I said I wouldn't say it. I said I wouldn't smoke.'

'Me and all,' said Geordie.

We giggled at each other.

'We'll go back to confession next week,' I said.

'Aye,' said Geordie. 'And then we'll really change.'

'Fishface!' we yelled. 'Fishface! Fishface!'

Then we calmed down and walked on and Geordie told me something new he'd picked up about Stephen Rose.

Eight

'He didn't leave,' he said.

'Eh?'

'Bennett College. The seminary. He didn't leave. They had to hoy him out.'

'Who says?'

'Me Uncle Joe.'

'Oh, your Uncle Joe?'

'I know, but he's not as daft as he looks. He met a bloke in the Columba Club that telt him the tale. They said Stephen Rose was an evil influence. They said there was some kind of devil worship involved. Black Masses and stuff. The Our Father backwards and upside-down crosses and black candles and stuff.'

'Ballocks. They wouldn't allow that in there.'

'But they didn't, did they? They chucked him out.'

'And the lads in there live in dormitories and there's priests looking after them day and night. We seen that when we went to play that football match against them.'

'There's always ways to do things, Davie. You know that.'

'Mebbe.'

'There was a couple of lads from Sunderland that was drove round the bend by it.'

'From Sunderland? Mebbe they deserved it, then.'

'Ha ha. They had to be sent out and all. And now they're in a special home in Rome and nuns look after them.'

I drew on me fag and pondered what he was saying.

'There had to be exorcism and stuff,' he said.

'You don't believe in that ballocks, do you?'

'What ballocks?'

'All that devil and exorcism stuff.'

'But if you believe in all the other stuff . . .'

'Like?'

'Like God and goodness. Then mebbe you got to believe in the devil and badness.'

'If you believe in anything at all.'

He put his hands on his hips and tilted his head and pursed his mouth.

'So now you're telling me you believe in nowt?' he said.

I shrugged.

'Mebbe I don't,' I said. 'Mebbe the whole lot of it's a load of nowt. Just a pack of crazy tales and lies and legends.'

I threw my cigarette away.

'That's ballocks,' he said. 'How can there not be nowt?'

'Dunno,' I said.

'Exactly. Just got to look around you.' He kicked a tree. 'You telling me this tree came from nowt? You're telling me the earth and the sky and the bliddy solar system came from nowt?' He poked my chest with his finger. 'You're telling me *you* came from nowt?'

'Dunno,' I said.

'Dunno? You're talking ballocks, man.'

I shrugged again. We walked on through the quiet streets.

'Anyway,' I said, 'if he's caused that much trouble, how come they're letting him come here and stay with somebody like Crazy bliddy Mary?'

'Aha, that's the other bit. He's been sent here cos of Father O'Mahoney. They reckon he knows about lads and how to keep an eye on them. You watch. You'll see him in and out of Crazy's house all the time.'

'I don't know,' I said.

'It's why they're keeping him out of school, and all. They don't want him corrupting kids like us. And

Crazy Mary? Easy. It's cos they reckon she's just too daft to get affected by him.' He laughed. 'It all makes sense, you see?'

He shook his head.

'You're too innocent, Davie,' he said. 'That's your problem. You think everything's nice and everybody's nice. You're naive, man.'

'Nick off,' I said.

'Aye. All right. But you are, man. You're clever and that, but you're a simpleton.' He wobbled his eyes and made his voice go spooky. 'You do not see the wickedness that's in the world!'

I pulled my collar up against the night chill.

'Nick off,' I said again.

Geordie put his arm around me.

'Aye, all right,' he said. 'Course, the big question is, What really happened to his dad? And why'd his mam go mental?'

I closed my eyes and said nothing. He laughed and pulled me tight. I felt the excitement burning in him.

'Poor Mouldy, eh?' he said. 'If only he knew what's waiting for him. Here, have another fag.'

Nine

Dinnertime a few days later. I played football with the lads on the school field, then I was heading back into school with the sweat dripping off me and a big rip in my trousers when a lass called Frances Malone came up and pretended to stumble into me.

She stood right up close to me.

'I know somebody that fancies you,' she said.

I said nowt.

'Well, go on,' she said. 'Ask me who.'

I wiped a drip of sweat away.

'Who?' I said.

'Not telling.'

'OK,' I said.

I wiped more sweat away. There were kids shoving past us to get to their lessons. There were teachers yelling for everybody to hurry up. I started to move on.

'Do you not care?' she said.

I shook my head. My heart was thumping.

'I know you do,' she said. 'You do, don't you?'

I said nothing. I moved away. She caught me up.

'Maria O'Callaghan,' she said. 'She thinks you're gorgeous. She says will you go with her.'

My heart jumped and jumped. I said nothing. She might be just taking the mick. I moved on.

'I bet you want to,' said Frances. 'I bet you think she's gorgeous. All the lads do.'

She giggled as I hurried on.

'Or do you just want to stay with that daft Geordie?' she called.

We had Art that afternoon. We got it from Prat Parker that had hair drooping down over his eyes and a stupid skimpy beard. Prat was all right, but he really was a prat. He used to fling his arms about and blather on about creativity and how art was a mix of crazy wildness and tough discipline. Then he'd give out sheets of paper and put flowers and pots and animal skulls and stuff in front of us and tell us, 'Draw what you see . . .' then he'd hold his finger up and his eyes would get wide like he was saying something dead profound, '. . . but do your seeing with the eyes of the imagination. Off you go, my artists!'

Usually Geordie and I messed about and splashed paint and flicked it and gave our pictures names like

The Message or *The Inner Blossom* or *Chaos* or *Dark Night of the Sole*. Prat thought they were brilliant. He thought they showed great promise. 'Perhaps a little too much freedom, though,' he said. 'I suggest you need to attend to boring accuracies before you fly so swiftly into fantasy. Lovely things, though. Lovely lovely things.' And he kept sticking them up on the wall.

This afternoon, though, he seemed dead calm. He said he had something quite wonderful to show us, and he put a couple of clay models on his table. I knew them straight away. Apostles.

'These were brought to me by Father O'Mahoney,' said Prat. 'They've been in the kiln overnight. They were made by a boy not much older than you are. And they are, quite simply . . . astonishing.'

Geordie looked at me. I looked at Geordie. We were dead proud. These things had started off as sloppy lumps of muck from our pond.

Prat told us to gather round. He told us to see how lifelike they were, how graceful, how beautifully formed.

'And yet they're so ordinary,' he said. 'Look at these faces. These aren't idealised heavenly beings. You could almost imagine them walking the streets of Felling. And they have an inner grace, an inner . . . light. Can you see this?'

Some of us murmured. A couple of us sniggered. Somebody farted. A paper plane curved through the air over our heads. Prat ignored it all.

'There are flaws, of course,' he said. 'A clumsiness in the shoulder there, a careless positioning of this ear. But art is not, and never has been, about perfection.'

He lifted one of them, turned it in his hands.

'Had I been told that they were the work of a thirty-year-old professional, I would not have been surprised.' He looked into our eyes. 'But for them to be the work of a boy, a boy who by all accounts – and I cannot expand – is in a condition of distress. Well, it is humbling. These are living things. Clay. Stone. Things of the earth. But alive!'

Then he put them away. He lifted a heavy bag of clay to his table.

'Now let us all,' he said, 'in our clumsy human way, begin to seek that inner light.'

Ten

That evening when we went to the cave we found Stephen sitting there. He was making a clay figure on his lap. A little fire was burning at his side. He looked up and saw us but he just looked down again and didn't speak.

'We seen your two apostles,' said Geordie.

'The art teacher showed us,' I said. 'He's called Prat. He said they were bloody brilliant.'

Stephen worked on.

'Smoke?' said Geordie.

He took a couple of Capstan out of his shirt pocket and held them out.

'Disgusting things,' said Stephen. 'They fill you with filth.'

'Aye?' said Geordie. He coughed and spat as he lit one up. 'They're lovely, though. Who's that one, then? St Buggerlugs?'

'St Peter.'

Geordie pointed to the pond.

'There's tons more where that come from. The clay gans right down to the middle of the world.'

Stephen looked at him.

'No, it doesn't,' he said. 'A boy come.'

'What? Here?'

'Aye.'

'How big was he?'

'Small. Kind of like me. But a thin and pointy thing.'

Me and Geordie looked at each other.

'Skinner,' I said. 'What did he say?'

'Nowt. He said he'd heard there were more of us. He said I should be careful who I joined up with.'

'What did you say?' said Geordie.

'Nowt. I told him to be gone. I showed him me knife. He went away.'

He picked up a beetle that was crawling across his foot. He looked at it, then crushed it with his thumb then lifted it up like he was waiting for it to do something.

'Where's it gone?' he said.

'Eh?' said Geordie.

'Nowt,' said Stephen.

He dropped the beetle into the fire and there was a quick little fizz as it burned.

'You do it just like that,' he said.

He looked around him.

'Saints used to live in caves like this,' he said. 'In the desert. In the wilderness. They tested themselves.'

'That's right,' said Geordie. 'Like that skinny bloke that ate all the locusts and that. And the one that never wore no clothes.'

'Aye,' said Stephen.

He smoothed the soft wet figure with his palm.

'At Bennett,' he said, 'a priest once said that mebbe I was more suited to the wilderness than to the civilised world.'

'Felling's the right place for you, then,' said Geordie.

'What happened there?' I said. 'At Bennett?'

Stephen shrugged.

'We learned the Catechism,' he said. 'We said prayers. We went to Mass. We ate loads of jam and bread. We did the ordinary school stuff – sums and English and Geography and stuff. Then we learned about God and miracles and how to be a good priest. There was football and cross-countries through the woods. Lots of lads seemed happy there.'

'Looked canny when we went,' said Geordie. 'Loads of mates. No mothers and sisters getting on your back.'

'Didn't suit all of us,' said Stephen. 'Some of us couldn't fit in.'

Geordie and I sat on stones near him. We smoked and looked at each other and said nowt and there was just the birds singing and the breeze rustling the leaves in Braddock's Garden and the scratching somewhere of tiny beasts. Far away, traffic droned on the by-pass. I dropped more sticks on to the flames. Stephen's fingers slipped across the clay. He kept looking up at me, like he was inspecting me. Between his hands, another lovely figure formed.

'It was winter when I went away,' he said. 'A taxi come for me. There were three other lads in it and a priest. I left me mam and dad at the front door. Me mam was crying. It didn't seem far. Not even an hour away. The college was ancient. Bare trees and empty fields all around it. We went in the gate and passed a pond and one of the kids said that's where we'd practise walking on water and the priest said aye, that was right. It was already dark when he took us in through the door.'

He looked up. It was darkening here as well. Sky getting red, the edge of the quarry dark and jagged against it.

'There were lads and priests everywhere,' he said. 'The smell of piss and incense and the sound of kids singing hymns.'

'Did it feel holy?' I said.

He glanced at me.

'Aye, Davie. It seemed dead holy.'

'Did you cry?' said Geordie.

'Eh?'

'Like on the first night in your bed. Did you miss your mam and dad and that?'

'No,' said Stephen. 'The new ones often wept and wailed, but not me. Aye, I mebbe missed me mam and dad at first. But I'd moved on. I thought there was work I had to do, and I couldn't do it if I stayed with them. When I went to Bennett, it was like I'd left an old life behind. It turned out I hadn't.'

Geordie and I smoked another Capstan.

'How did you know in the first place?' said Geordie.

'Know what?'

'That you wanted to be a priest.'

He shrugged. He stared into the sky.

'I knew soon after the angel came,' he said.

'The angel?' said Geordie. 'What bliddy angel?'

'Tell you in a minute,' said Stephen. Then he leaned closer to Geordie. 'Anyway, what do you want to be?'

'Me?' said Geordie. 'Dunno. A footballer! Newcastle for ever!'

Stephen turned his eyes to me.

'What about you?' he said.

I shrugged.

'A footballer as well,' I said.

He shook his head like he was disappointed.

'You tell lies, Davie, don't you?'

'What?'

'It's OK. We all do. Sometimes lies can help you. Me, I always knew I was going to do something special. I always knew there was something lying in wait for me.'

He paused and looked at me.

'Do you not feel like that?' he said.

I shook my head quickly.

'No?' he said. 'Do you not think there's a special purpose to your life?'

I shook my head again.

He raised his eyebrows, like he didn't believe me.

'What about the angel?' said Geordie.

'Aye,' said Stephen. 'She struck me down and lifted me up again and everything was changed.'

He licked his lips as we leaned close to him. He rolled clay between his finger and thumb and I saw an arm appearing before me.

'What d'you mean?' I said.

Eleven

Stephen paused and breathed slowly, like he was gathering the tale into himself before he told it to us. He worked his clay with his fingers. He carved its features with the point of a knife. It grew more lifelike as he spoke.

'It was a Tuesday morning. I was down on the beach at Whitley Bay. I was walking all alone like always. It was boiling hot. There was people all around me. People lying flat out in the sun. Screaming kids and yapping dogs splashing in the water. The smell of chips and hot dogs and coffee. Just ordinary, dead ordinary. Then there come a hush. Dead silence, nowt moving, like everything was stopped in time. Then a blast come from the sky and it was like a bolt of lightning went right through me. I found meself crawling on the sand. I was weak as a baby. I could hardly breathe. And there she was.'

'Bliddy Hell,' said Geordie.

'Aye,' said Stephen. 'She was in the sky over the cliffs with massive wings and a sword in her hand and she was that bright, bright as the sun, bright and burning and I turned me face away from her. "Stephen Rose!" she yelled. "Stephen Rose! You cannot hide!" And it was like her voice was everywhere, outside me and inside me. I couldn't do nowt. I had to turn. She come down towards me. She pointed the sword at me. "Who is thy lord, Stephen Rose?" she said. "Answer! For you cannot hide. Who is thy lord?" And I knew what I had to say. "My lord is God most high," I answered. And everything went dead still again, and dark as night, and I thought I must've died, and then the angel was at me side, and was helping me up, and the sword was hanging on its own in the sky, pointing down at us. "You have answered well," she whispered. And she took my hands in hers and hers were that tender and so strong. And she said, "With these hands, you must be about the Lord's work, Stephen Rose." And I felt the power growing in them. "Remember that thou art dust and dirt," she said, "and remember that thou art also holy." And she pulled me up till I stood on the sand and the sea started to move again and the folk and the dogs started to stir again. "I will watch thee, Stephen Rose," she whispered, "even unto the end of thy days.

Remember to use thy talents well." And she was gone.'

I looked at Geordie. Geordie looked at me.

'Did anybody else see her?' Geordie whispered.

'I was the only privileged one,' said Stephen. 'The sunbathers went on frying, the kids went on screaming, the dogs went on yapping, but for me, in an instant, everything had changed.'

'Bliddy Hell,' I said.

'Aye,' said Stephen. 'And she's been back a couple of times since.'

'Bliddy Hell,' said Geordie.

'Do you believe me?' said Stephen.

'Dunno,' I said.

'Dunno,' he echoed. He leaned close to me, looked into me. 'Some people find it hard to believe anything, Davie. They want proof. What if the angel came to you, Davie? Would you believe me then? Or would you still just say dunno? And what if you saw the power of the Lord himself at work here in Felling?'

He inspected the finished apostle.

'No need to be scared,' he said. 'Not yet.'

He held the apostle up in front of my eyes, and its face looked into my face. He smiled.

'But one day,' he said, 'I'll mebbe show you something that'll scare you stiff. It'll scatter all your doubts. There'll be no more maybes or dunnos.' He lowered his voice to a whisper. 'You'll be bliddy petrified, Davie. Your soul'll bliddy crack.'

He smiled. He winked at Geordie.

'Just joking,' he said, and he finished his tale. 'Soon after I was struck down and raised up again, a priest come to the school looking for vocations. I stood up. "Me," I said. "I'll be a priest." And pretty soon, off I went to Bennett.'

He laid the apostle at the centre of the fire. He heaped embers up around it. He placed more sticks to quicken the fire. I watched them burn.

Then we flinched and were dead still. There were footsteps above us, in Braddock's Garden.

Two silhouettes of boys appeared at the quarry's edge.

'Skinner,' I whispered.

'Aye,' said Geordie. 'And looks like Poke and all.'

'But not Mouldy, thank God.'

'These are your enemies?' said Stephen.

'Aye,' said Geordie.

We watched the boys crouch above us. They peered down. We heard them whispering. They moved around the quarry's rim. We heard them coming down towards the quarry's entrance. I hunched with Geordie in the shadows under the rock as they crept closer.

'See?' he whispered. 'If we had tripwires they'd be straight in the bliddy pond.'

'Get ready to jump and yell,' I said. 'We'll scare the living daylights out of them.'

We tried to hold our giggles in. We waited, but Stephen was the first to move. He slipped out of the cave and ran fast and low. There was a commotion under the hawthorn trees, then the Pelaw lads started squealing. We heard them crashing away. Then Skinner's voice, weeping with fright.

'He stabbed me! He bliddy stabbed me!'

Then Poke, yelling down from the quarry's rim:

'Wait till we tell Mouldy!'

Twelve

Stephen came back, wiping his knife-blade on a handful of grass. We were trembling. We were speechless. We started backing away.

'What's *wrong*?' said Stephen. 'It's just a scratch. A little warning.'

He grinned at us.

'I thought you hated them. And who's this Mouldy?'

We just looked at him.

'Who's *Mouldy*?' he repeated.

He shrugged.

'Don't tell me, then,' he said.

He knelt in front of the fire. He spat and the spit hissed. Geordie cursed under his breath, then found his voice.

'Mouldy,' he said, 'is Martin Mould. He's just the hardest bugger for miles around.'

'Is that right, Davie?' said Stephen.

'Aye,' I said.

'And Mouldy,' said Geordie, 'is their mate. He is hard as nails. He is massive. He is a bliddy monster. And he'll kill you now. And us and all.'

'Is that right, Davie?' said Stephen again.

'Aye.'

'Oh, dear,' he said. 'What have I done?'

He goggled and pretended to scream and tremble.

'A monster!' he said. 'I'm so scared!'

'Stupid git,' muttered Geordie.

Stephen knelt with his face glowing above the fire. The embers round the apostle flickered in the dusk. Stephen stirred them with a stick. He scratched the embers away from the figure.

'Howay,' I whispered to Geordie.

But I looked down, and I was caught by the face staring out from the fire.

'Are you done yet, my apostle?' said Stephen. He poked it with his stick. 'Are you ready to come and rescue us?'

He stood up and his head was silhouetted against the moon. He spread his arms. He held the stick high above his head. He lowered it quickly and pointed to the fire.

'Stand up,' he said. 'Stand up, my apostle. Walk the earth. Save us from our tormentors. I command you. Walk!'

Geordie and I kept backing away. Stephen laughed.

'No,' he said. 'He's not done yet. Needs a bit more cooking.'

He shoved the embers back. He threw more sticks on and he laughed.

'Take no notice,' he said. 'It's just me being daft. So this Martin Mould's a monster, then?'

We said nothing.

'And you're scared of him and you hate his guts?'

We said nothing. Stephen smiled through the dusk and the firelight.

'You know,' he said, 'the world'd be a much better place without a thing like Mouldy. Do you think so?'

We said nothing.

'Aye?' he said.

'Aye,' said Geordie.

Stephen turned his eyes to me.

'Aye, Davie?' he said.

I paused as he watched me. Then I shrugged and nodded.

'Aye.'

And we heard a voice echoing towards us, a thin hesitant wavery voice.

'Stephen! Stephen Rose! Where are you, Stephen Rose?'

'It's Crazy,' I said.

'The loony woman,' said Stephen. 'Better go or they'll be sending me away somewhere. And I don't want that, do I?' He looked into my eyes. 'Not when there's so much to do here.'

Then he slipped away.

'*He's* the loony,' said Geordie. 'We got to let Mouldy know he's nowt to do with us.'

'He'll take no notice of that,' I said.

I felt Mouldy's hands on my throat, his boot on my face.

'Let's go,' I said, and we hurried out.

Next morning I woke dead early. I left the house early. I went into the quarry. There'd been a frost. The clay pond had a fringe of ice. I crouched over the embers. I pulled away the ash and cinders. He was lying there, filthy, black with ash, hard as stone. The last heat of the fire was still in him, but very soon he'd be bitter cold. I cleaned his face with spit: a calm and ordinary face, a Felling face. He could be any passer-by. Then my heart stood still. The clay figure was me. It was my face that looked up at me from between my own hands.

I trembled. I crossed myself. I closed my eyes.

'Deliver us from evil,' I prayed.

Two

Thirteen

'So which one is it?' said Dad. 'Her on the left or her on the right? Her that keeps looking in or her that keeps not looking in? Her that . . .'

I sighed. We were sitting at the table eating eggy bread and drinking tea. The lasses must have walked past the window half a dozen times. Frances kept looking in and pretending she wasn't looking in. Maria kept pretending there was something fascinating high up in the sky. The pair of them were linked arm in arm. They were giggling and grinning.

'The brunette or the blonde?' said Dad.

'Frances or Maria?' said Mam.

Dad laughed.

'And which one's got the eye for Geordie?'

They walked by again. Dad kept on nudging and asking. I kept on eating, drinking and pretending not to watch for them. Then they were gone.

'Lost your chance,' said Dad.

'I'm not interested,' I said.

'Oh, aye?' he said.

'Well, they're both nice girls by all accounts,' said Mam.

Dad laughed.

'Your mother knows and sees everything,' he said.

She slapped another slice on to my plate.

'But mind don't you go running after them,' she said. 'There's time enough for that. Go and kick a ball or something with Geordie.'

When I went out, they were at the end of the street, in the cut between the houses. I slowed down when I got close to them. We all pretended we were invisible but just as I was passing by, Frances said,

'Not speaking?'

'Aye,' I said.

'Gan on, then,' she said.

'Gan on what?'

'Speak.'

'Hello,' I said.

'Hello,' she said. 'And what about Maria?'

I tried to still my heart and calm my breath.

'Hello,' I said.

Maria bit her lips and blushed and looked sideways at me.

'Hello,' she said.

We looked at each other, then we couldn't do it any more. Maria walked away. Frances laughed and said, 'Well, it's a start,' and she followed Maria, and I went through another cut to get to Geordie.

He was in his back garden. His old knife-throwing door was leaning on the hedge like always. It had the outline of a body painted on it. He'd been chucking his knife at it like always, trying just to miss the body. There were hundreds of marks on the body and head where he and his dad had missed over the years. He passed the knife to me when I walked in.

'Gan on,' he said. 'You have a go, Davie. I can't do nowt today.'

I took the knife. I aimed for the edge of the door. I chucked it. It glittered in the sun then thudded right in where the body's heart would be.

'Ballocks,' I said.

'Bull's-eye!' yelled Geordie's dad from inside. 'Get that lad straight into the circus!'

I slumped down into the grass.

'What we going to do?' I said. 'Mouldy'll be out for revenge.'

'God knows,' said Geordie. 'I dreamed about him last night.'

'Did you?'

'Aye. He stabbed us both then cooked us in a big pot down in the quarry.'

'Honest?'

'Honest. He had us with toast and HP Sauce.'

'Bliddy Hell.'

'And a big bottle of Tizer.'

We knew there was nothing funny but we couldn't help but laugh.

'Mebbe we should tell our dads,' I said.

'It's a battle we made for ourselves. That's what *my* dad would say.'

'I know. But when there's a knife involved, Geordie . . .'

'Crazy bliddy Stephen Rose's knife. Not ours.'

'I know.'

'We'll sort it out ourselves. We need to fix a meeting.'

'With Mouldy?'

'Aye. Him and the others. We'll just tell him all about Stephen Rose. We'll tell him it'll never happen again.'

'Bliddy Hell. Mouldy cannot hardly even talk, man.'

'He cannot be that thick.'

'Can he not? Remember that story about him biting rats' heads off down in Jonadab?'

'Aye. I remember. And the one about him biting that kid's lug off in Jarrow.'

We said nowt else for a while while we thought of that.

'Did you believe it?' said Geordie at last.

'Aye,' I said.

'So did I.'

We sat against the door. Inside the house, Geordie's dad danced about and yelled out, 'The times they are a-changing!'

'What a racket,' I said.

'Do you want to go to the cave?' said Geordie.

I shook my head.

'Me, neither,' said Geordie.

There seemed nowt we could do. I closed my eyes and let the sun fall on my face. I felt the grass warm against my fingers. I listened to the birds. I thought of the spring coming on so fast. I found myself drifting, dreaming about the apostle in the fire. He stood up and stretched himself and stepped away from the ashes. Newborn tiny frogs gathered around him from the pond. A grass snake curled up at his side on a stone. The sparrowhawk wheeled high above. Stephen came, creeping beneath the hawthorn. 'Where are you?' he whispered. 'Are you done yet?' He crept closer. 'Where are you? Are you done yet, Davie?'

I shook myself awake. Geordie's sister Noreen was at

the back door, leaning on the frame, smiling. She narrowed her eyes. She tapped her cheek.

'So what you two been up to?' she said.

'Nowt for you,' said Geordie.

She shook her head and laughed.

'You're still just little boys, aren't you?' she said. 'Just silly little . . .'

Geordie put two fingers up.

'Get lost!' he hissed.

She just laughed again. She ran her fingers through her hair and wiggled her hips as she went back inside.

'Lasses!' said Geordie.

'There's a lass says she fancies me,' I said.

'Aye?' said Geordie.

'Aye.'

He stared at me, then he slouched back into the grass.

'That's all we bliddy need.'

74

Fourteen

The moon was huge, right at the middle of my window. It was round as a communion host. I lay there in its light. I stared into its face. I made out its craters, its waterless seas. I heard a voice.

'Davie! Davie!'

Was I hearing things?

'Davie! Davie!'

A rattle at my window like tiny pebbles, grit.

'Davie! Davie! Davie!'

I went to the window and stared out and there he was. Stephen Rose, face like wax, reflecting the moon. He raised his hand. He beckoned me. I shivered. I drew the curtains. I went back to my bed.

I lay and tried to sleep. His voice went on for a while, then stopped, then started again, but this time it seemed close by me in my room, it seemed to echo from deep inside my head.

'Davie! Davie! Davie!'

I felt Stephen's fingers on me, like he was forming me, like I was his clay. His fingers slid and slipped across me. I squirmed on the bed, trying to break free from him.

'Be still,' he whispered. 'Let me make you, Davie.'

I blocked my ears with my hands.

'You're mine, Davie,' he whispered.

I clenched my fists, gritted my teeth.

'No,' I said. 'No!'

'Who is thy lord, Davie? You cannot hide. Who is thy lord?'

'Get off me! Let me go!'

And then there was just stillness and silence outside me and inside me.

My bedroom door opened. Mam came in.

'Davie?' she whispered. 'Are you OK, Davie?'

I curled towards her.

'Aye,' I said. 'Aye, Mam.'

'Bad dream?' she said.

'Aye. Aye . . .'

She put her gentle hand on my brow. She soothed me with her fingers.

'Now sleep, Davie. That's right. Just go back to sleep.'

And she pulled the curtain, blocking out the moon.

Fifteen

Next day we were walking home from school when Geordie saw Mouldy leaving The Swan.

'Mouldy!' he gasped.

'Where?'

'And he's bliddy seen us!'

Mouldy started running for us. Geordie yanked my arm and dragged me after him. Mouldy had to run uphill but still he was catching us. I dared to look and I saw his massive body, vicious face, pumping arms, fast thundering feet.

'Mother of God,' I prayed.

He got closer, closer.

'Oh, Hell,' I gasped.

He growled, grunted, snarled. I could smell the beer from his breath. I waited for him to kick my legs away. I waited for the first thump of his fist on my back. I felt his fingers as he tried to grab me. I leaped forward, ran faster.

'Crazy Mary's,' said Geordie, and we swerved towards her garden. We ran to her door and hammered on it. Nobody came, but Mouldy hesitated at the gate. He glared, red-faced, dark-eyed. He stamped like a beast.

'We know the people here,' said Geordie. 'They'll set the police on you.'

Mouldy came on again, slower now. He licked his lips and bared his teeth. 'Don't, Mouldy,' I said. I clenched my fists. I looked down, seeking a rock, a stone, any kind of weapon. Then Crazy came and the door inched open. We shoved our way inside and slammed it shut. We backed against the wall. The letter box swung open. Mouldy glared through. His eyes goggled in at us. I found Stephen at my side.

'So that's your monster out there?' he said.

'Aye,' I said.

He had a handful of ash. He threw it into Mouldy's eyes.

'Go to Hell!' he said.

Mouldy squealed and the letter box dropped shut. He battered with his feet and fists at the door.

Stephen laughed.

'Stupid lump,' he said, and he yelled at the door: 'The police is coming! They're on their way now! They are! They are! Begone!'

The battering went on for a while, then it relented,

and Mouldy spoke to us once more before he went away.

'You're dead,' he growled through the door. 'Every bliddy one of you.'

Crazy looked at us in confusion.

'But we're not,' she said.

She looked at us.

'Are we?' she said.

I shook my head. No.

I looked out through the letter box. Stephen stood beside me and looked out, too. We saw Mouldy lumbering back towards The Swan.

'Aye, scary,' said Stephen. 'But stupid as well.'

He wiped the ash from his hands. My terror started to fade.

'Such devils walk the streets these days,' said Crazy Mary.

'They do, Aunty Mary,' said Stephen.

'But these two is the good altar boys,' said Crazy Mary.

'We are, Missus,' said Geordie.

'Come and have some jam and bread,' said Crazy.

I dipped my fingers into Crazy's holy water and crossed myself. We went towards the back of the house. Crazy cut thick slices of bread. She spread them deeply with rhubarb jam.

'Eat,' she said. 'This is the good food of the Lord.'

Geordie and I looked at each other.

'Narrow escape, eh?' he said.

We both tried to laugh, but we both knew we'd been terrified.

I crammed the bread into my mouth.

Stephen watched, so calm.

'Davie,' he said. 'I've got something I want to show you.' He looked at Geordie. 'Not you,' he said. 'Just Davie. Is that OK?'

I saw the suspicion and anger in Geordie's eyes.

'I've just saved your bliddy life,' said Stephen. 'I'd like you to stay here.'

They watched each other for a moment. Then Geordie shrugged.

'We'll not be long,' said Stephen. 'Come and see, Davie.'

I hesitated. My heart was still thundering.

'Howay,' he said. 'You'll be interested.' He stepped towards the back door and opened it. 'Bring your jam and bread if you want to. Come with me, Davie.'

Sixteen

Crows flew out from the grass as he led me to the shed. He took me in, shut the door behind us.

'Forget the outside, Davie,' he said. 'Forget what you were scared of.'

The place was pale with clay dust. Dust on the bench top, the dark creosoted timber walls, on the window. Milky light fell on us.

'It's great stuff,' he said, 'the stuff I get from your pond. Slick and smooth, easy to work, like it wants to live.'

I shivered at the thought of ever going to the pond again. I shivered at the thought of Mouldy waiting beside it in the shadow of the rock.

'You're still thinking about Mouldy, aren't you?' he said. 'You're safe here, man.' He laughed. 'Mouldy! What a name, eh? Mouldy!' He licked his lips and laughed. 'Mouldy. That's what he will be when he's dead.'

There was clay in glass bowls with wet cloths over them. There were finished figures, half-formed figures. Stephen dipped his hand into a bowl of cloudy water and splashed it over them.

'Don't want them drying out too quick,' he said. 'Don't want them cracking and crazing, do we?'

He grinned and flicked water at me, too.

'Calm down, man,' he said. 'Everything's all right now.'

There were figures that were nearly formless. Just blocks of stone with lumps for arms and legs, and skulls like boulders balanced on top. He saw me watching.

'Mebbe God made things like these first,' he said. 'Before he got to us. Try-outs. Thick stupid lumpy things without a soul. What d'you think, Davie?'

'Dunno,' I said.

'Dunno,' he echoed. 'Mebbe there was a time of beasts and monsters before there came the time of us. Mebbe there's things like them things walking still. Mebbe there's things around us that was created by the devil and not by God. Things like the thing that snarled through the door at you. Things like your Mouldy.'

'Aye,' I said. 'Mebbe. Aye.'

He watched me.

'Or mebbe,' he said, 'the time of beasts and monsters is just about to start. What do you think, Davie?'

I shrugged, shook my head. I saw a fallen twisted crucifix among the clay. I reached down and tried to stand it up. I pressed it into a lump of soft clay to stop it falling.

'D'you ever think you might still want to be a priest?' I said.

'No. That's all over, Davie. There's other ways to live a life and serve the Lord.'

He drew one of the bowls towards himself. He took the wet cloth off. He ripped a little lump of clay away. He started shaping a human body with it. He paused.

'I wanted to do this last night with you,' he said. 'But you saw me and you didn't come down.' He grinned. 'Why not? Too scared to come out in the dark?'

I twisted my face, turned to go.

'Don't be stupid,' I said.

'Now the thing called Mouldy's drove you here,' he went on. 'It's nearly like there was a purpose to it . . . You'll not tell nobody.'

'Eh?'

'You'll not tell nobody what's going on in here.'

I looked back at him. What was there to tell? I watched the dust tumbling through the light, gathering on us. I watched the clay figure taking shape between his hands.

'Don't go just yet,' he said. 'Watch this.'

The figure was tiny, delicate, half-formed, not like the other formless soulless lumps, but like a baby, half-made.

'Move,' he whispered to it. 'Move, my little one.'

He sighed and smiled.

'There. Did you see, Davie?'

'See what?'

He breathed the words again.

'Move. Live, little one. See?'

I moved closer, gazed down. There was nothing.

Stephen held the child in one hand, and stared at me. He passed his other hand before my eyes once, twice, then again.

'Look again,' he whispered. I looked down into his hands, to the baby lying there. 'Move,' he whispered. 'Live!'

He sighed with pleasure.

'Look, Davie,' he said. 'Look deep. Look with the eyes of the spirit, Davie. When I say you'll see it move, you will see it move.'

He lifted the child towards me. He passed his hand before my eyes again.

'Now, Davie,' he whispered. 'You will see it move.'

And I did see, and I nearly cried out with fright, but he stopped it dead. He dropped the child on to the bench, clapped his hand across my mouth.

'You got to tell nobody, Davie,' he said. 'You got to promise me. Promise me now.'

I goggled back into his eyes. I nodded. I reached out and touched the child. It was cold stiff clay, nothing more.

'Do you see what we're capable of?' he whispered. 'You and me, Davie? You should forget about your friends and . . .'

Then there were footsteps outside, and he quickly moved back from me.

'Remember,' he said. 'Tell nobody nothing! Tell them nowt!'

Seventeen

There was a knock at the shed door, then Father O'Mahoney came in. He stood there tall beside us in his black suit with the single band of white around his throat. His coppery hair gleamed. There was a scent of incense on him.

'Now then, lads,' he said.

'Hello, Father,' I said.

'Aye aye, Davie. You've found a couple of pals for yourself, then, Stephen.'

Stephen smiled.

'Yes, Father.'

'That's grand.'

The priest ran a finger through the dust on the bench. He straightened the crucifix. He lifted the baby.

'There's an artist come among us, Davie. Did you ever see the like of these grand things?'

'No, Father.'

'Indeed no. God lavishes his gifts on some. Thanks be.'

He crossed himself. He allowed his gaze to linger on me.

'Are you all right, Davie?'

'Aye, Father. Yes.'

'Nothing troubling you?'

'No, Father.'

He rested his open hand on my head for a moment.

'To some God gives a true and simple heart,' he said. 'Do you see that, Stephen?'

'I do,' said Stephen.

'There are some who would make use of such a thing. Who would exploit it.'

'I know that, Father. Davie'll be a good friend for me, Father.'

The priest clasped his hands and nodded at the two of us.

'That's grand,' he said. 'That's just what I would hope. We must care for each other in our time on earth. It is the simplest of things and the most difficult of things.'

He lifted up the kneeling figure of an angel. 'Just look at this!' he breathed in admiration. He tapped his cheek, deep in thought.

'Would you like me to go, Father?' I said.

He laughed, as if he'd been brought back to his senses.

'Ha! Indeed no. That is if Stephen doesn't mind discussion of some private matters before you.'

Stephen shook his head.

'That's grand. He should know which way the land lies if he's to be a pal of yours. So. I come from a visit to your mother, Stephen.'

Stephen's face fell.

'Do you?' he whispered.

'Indeed,' said the priest. He turned to me. 'Your pal's mother has been very ill, Davie. You must know that. And you must also know some of the tittle-tattle that surrounds it. You must take no notice of that. Some of us, like Stephen's mother, are tested much more severely than others are.'

'How is she?' whispered Stephen.

The priest sighed.

'A little better, I believe. We prayed together. I ministered communion to her. We talked a little of Whitley Bay and the beaches there. Ha! She told me about ice creams and bags of chips and spinning on the roundabouts when she was a little girl. It sounded so grand!'

'Did she mention me?' said Stephen.

'Ah, now.'

'Did she?'

'She is distracted, Stephen. She sleeps a great deal. She is calm. The medication does its work.' He tried to rest his hand on Stephen's shoulder, but Stephen shrugged it off. 'And she will come out of it, my son. Very soon, perhaps. They thought they could assure me of that.'

Silence again. Stephen stared blankly at the floor. The dust fell on him. The priest stood close by his side.

'We must remember, I suppose,' he said, 'that the Lord himself was tested more than any other.'

He glanced up through the glass and shook his head. He murmured a quick prayer over Stephen's head.

'This is all private stuff, now, Davie,' he said. 'You understand that?'

'Aye, Father.'

'That's grand.' He rubbed his hands together. 'And now,' he said, 'I believe your good Aunt Mary was about to put a kettle on.'

He opened the door, stepped out, then leaned back in again.

'Aha!' he said. He winked at Stephen. 'Nearly forgot. I heard somebody giggling about your new pal, Stephen.'

We said nothing.

'I did. A nice lass named . . . ah, it's slipped my mind.'
He winked again. 'Soon they'll all be after him. And
after you as well, eh? You just watch.'

He raised his hand.

'Don't worry, Stephen,' he said. 'You'll be grand here.
An ordinary life, with good ordinary folk around
you . . .'

He moved his hand through the air and blessed us
and was gone.

'Stupid sod!' hissed Stephen. 'He's what they wanted
to turn us into at Bennett.' He mocked the priest's
voice.' "You'll be grand here. An ordinary life. Ordinary
folk." Cretin.'

He lifted the angel and flung it at the floor.

'You don't know him,' I said. 'He's—'

'Damn him!' he said. 'Damn his bliddy ordinariness.
Damn it all!'

He glared. His eyes shone with tears and rage. He
caught my arm as I turned away.

'And damn me mother and all,' he said. 'If she had
her way she'd have me bliddy dead!'

'That can't be true.'

'Can it not? How do you know?'

He started to cry.

'Tell nobody!' he said. 'Bliddy nobody! Nobody!'

He lifted the baby up again. He glared at it.

'Live!' he snapped. 'Move, you stupid object! Live!'

It squirmed in his cupped hands. I closed my eyes, opened them. It was still again. He pinched jagged little wings into its back. He pinched a jagged tail into it. He raised it to his lips, whispered to it.

'Damn them all,' he said.

Its wings started to open. It raised its head. It seemed about to take flight. Then Stephen flung it at the angel on the floor.

I picked it up. I held it and watched it and watched Stephen.

'How do you do it?' I said.

'It?' he said. 'It is nowt. It's a piece of bliddy cake. But one day I'll do something that's really something. I'll make a proper monster. I'll make a thick stupid vicious thing without a soul. There'll be death and doom and murder, Davie. D'you believe me?'

I looked at the angel on the floor, at the devil in my hands. Had I really seen what I thought I'd seen?

'No,' I said.

'No?' He laughed at me. 'After everything you've just seen, you say no?'

I nodded. I shrugged. I shook my head.

'Yes. No. How do I know?' Then I looked him in the face. He was just a kid, just like us. 'No,' I said. 'I don't believe it.'

He took the devil away from me. He held it like he was going to command it to move again, then he crushed it to a simple lump of clay.

'OK,' he said. 'Let's doubt, let's say no, let's not believe.'

'OK,' I said.

I stood there watching him. The dust tumbled through the light between us. I knew I didn't want to leave. I knew I wanted to see it again – moving clay, living clay.

'What you waiting for?' he said. 'It didn't happen. You were deceived. You must have been.'

I went into the daylight, then to Father O'Mahoney and Crazy Mary drinking tea and Geordie sitting with them trying to be polite. He stood straight up when he saw me. The priest raised his hand, went on murmuring to Mary. Geordie and I went out into Felling's streets. Geordie breathed a massive sigh of relief.

'What I need is a tab,' he said.

We slumped on the bench on Watermill Lane and smoked Senior Service and stared down to The Swan.

'So what was all that in the shed?' he said.

I looked at him.

'Nowt,' I said.

He looked at me.

'What's up with you?' he said.

'Nowt,' I said.

He kept looking.

'Nowt, man!' I said.

He shrugged and smoked.

'OK,' he said.

But he kept on looking.

Eighteen

All week, clay babies crawled and whimpered in my dreams. Little devils with stunted wings strutted and cackled and flew. I told myself I was wrong. I must have been. Like Stephen said, I'd been deceived. It was all illusion. I thought of God making us. I wondered if artists were like God, if they had a bit of God inside themselves. I wondered, is it only God who can breathe life into the world, only God who can create? I kept recalling Stephen's voice. *Move. Live.* And I kept recalling what I'd seen before my eyes.

Prat brought bags of clay into his lesson that week. I moulded lumps of it between my hands. It was cold and gritty stuff. It wouldn't take the lovely shapes I wanted it to take. Just stupid clumsy hopeless things appeared between my hands. I looked at Stephen's beautiful apostles standing on a shelf. I watched Geordie quickly extruding arms and legs, eyes on stalks, forming scales and claws. I watched him make a multi-limbed disgusting thing. Prat held it up to show it to the rest of us. Such a bold exciting piece, he said. A thing from deep down in the dark, a true true monster.

He laughed.

'Some would say, of course,' he said, 'that what the artist does, is to give an outer form to his inner self.'

And he held the monster's face by Geordie's face and gasped in horror at the similarity. I caught Maria looking at me. She held up a thing that was becoming a horse and pretended to race it through the air in front of her. She smiled at me. I raised my hand.

'Sir,' I said.

'Yes, Davie?'

I tried to form the question.

'Do you think,' I said, 'that an artist is a kind of God?'

'Aha!' Prat flicked his hair back. He tugged at his scrawny beard and pondered. He suddenly reached up to a shelf behind him and pulled a dusty Bible down.

'And the Lord God formed man of the dust of the ground,' he read, 'and breathed into his nostrils the breath of life; and man became a living soul.'

He closed the book. He walked back and forward before us with his chin in his hand.

'We are certainly copying him in some way,' he said. Some of the kids were throwing clay about. Prat didn't even notice, or he pretended not to notice, when a little bit of it just missed his head and smacked into the blackboard.

'But is human creativity equal to the creativity of God?' he said. 'That question has led many down a darkening and ever more terrifying path. What would our priests say to such a question? At one time their answers might have involved boiling oil and thumbscrews and racks.' He smiled at Geordie's monster. 'No, Davie,' he said, and he addressed all of us. 'I think an artist is simply human, a human with an astounding skill, a skill that may indeed be God-given, but nevertheless . . . human.' He gently handed Geordie his monster back. 'We cannot, like God, create a soul. We cannot, like God, create life. But who is to say what the limits of our creativity might nevertheless be?'

Geordie poked and pulled at the clay while Prat blathered on. He blew into his monster's horrible mouth. He held it up and rocked it in his hand and grunted,

'Hello, Davie. Me gonna eat you up.'

Maria jogged her horse across her bench. She kept on smiling at me.

When Prat shut up, Geordie nudged me, dead chuffed.

'You'll never guess what I've done,' he said.

'You're right,' I said. 'I'll never guess.'

'I've sorted out a meeting with Mouldy,' he said.

'You're joking.'

'Na. I seen Skinner. We sorted it out. Tuesday night. There'll be a truce.'

'A meeting? With that . . .'

'I telt him Stephen Rose is a bliddy lunatic. I telt him about his mother in the nuthouse and that. I telt him even if he is a Catholic and he lives in Felling he's nowt to do with us.'

'Is he not?'

'Course he's not. I said I'd ploat him meself if it wasn't for the priest.'

'And a meeting with bliddy. . .'

'I know, but Skinner says he's not that bad, really. He says there's a soft side to him.'

I just looked at him. He grinned.

'There's a good side to everybody, man,' he said. 'I've heard you say it yourself.'

I couldn't say anything.

'And he's had a really tough life,' Geordie said.

'Who has?'

'Mouldy, man.'

'I feel really sorry for him, then.'

Geordie laughed.

'Aye,' he said. 'The poor troubled soul.'

I grunted, and fiddled with my clay. I rolled it between my palms and the bench top and made a stupid wormy shape. I thought of the baby squirming in Stephen's hands. I thought of the way he whispered to it to move and live.

Geordie held his monster up.

'Hello, Davieboy,' it growled. 'Me is hungry.'

I shook my head and sighed.

'Worry not,' it said. 'Me will protect you from horrible Mouldy. Ugh. Ugh.'

Prat urged us on.

'Don't stop, my artists! Astounding things might lie in wait!'

Nineteen

We served at a wedding that Saturday. It was a lass from Leam Lane called Vera that'd left school just a couple of years back and a scrawny little bloke called Billy White. Geordie reckoned Vera must be up the stick to marry an ugly bloke like him but I couldn't see a bump. There was thunder during the service. You could see all the aunties and neighbours in the congregation staring up at the roof and worrying about their hats. By the time they went out for the photographs, though, the storm had gone and everything was drying. They all stood in the sun beside the statue of St Patrick in his animal skins and with his wild long hair and with snakes squirming under his feet. Then the blokes in the families loosened their ties and smoked and joked and laughed. The women talked about each other's hats and kept screaming at something hilarious. Kids belted up and down the church steps. Father O'Mahoney chatted and smiled. Me and Geordie eyed the guests up and wondered where the tip might come from. I saw Maria there, standing with the women, looking bored. Then Billy White called us over. He said Vera wanted a picture of us beside them in our cassocks and cottas. A memento, he said. So they could remember everything about their perfect day. Would we mind? We shrugged. All right, we said. I said Geordie'd probably bust the camera, though. We stood there with the bride and groom between us. We joined our hands together and raised our eyes to Heaven. There were great fluffy white clouds in the icy blue sky and I felt like I was toppling over as my eyes followed them. There was a click and a flash then Billy shook our hands. He said he and Vera would be honoured if we accepted a little token and he held out a ten-bob note to us. Geordie shoved it in his pocket.

'Ten bob!' we whispered.

'I telt you that Billy was a good bloke,' said Geordie.

Then they took a photo with Father O'Mahoney standing at their side with his hand raised in blessing.

We were just going back up the steps into church to take our altar gear off when Maria came over.

'She looks lovely, doesn't she?' she said.

I stopped on the second step. Geordie kept climbing. I gulped. I looked past Maria to Vera.

'Aye,' I said.

'She's me cousin. She must be daft, though, eh?'

'Eh?'

'Getting married, at her age. You won't find me doing that.'

'Won't you?'

'Na. You won't find me getting trapped. I'll be off into the wild blue yonder!'

I looked at Billy cuddling and kissing Vera beside the statue. Maria grinned at me. She shrugged.

'That's all,' she said. 'Just thought I'd come and say hello.'

'Hello,' I said. Her eyes were lovely, bluer than the sky. 'I liked your horse,' I said as she turned away.

'What horse?'

'The one you made in Prat's class.'

She put her hands on her hips.

'That horse, Davie, was a lion.'

She grinned, then we looked away from each other. The women in the hats were howling their heads off again.

'I'm not going to the reception,' she said.

'Oh.'

'It'll be all ham sandwiches and squealing brats and blokes puking up around the back.'

She looked at the sky.

'It's a lovely day for a walk,' she said.

'Is it?' I said.

'D'you want to go for one?'

I could feel Geordie urging me to get away from her. She looked up at him, rolled her eyes, looked back at me.

'Do you?' she said.

'Aye.'

'I'll wait for you out here, then,' she said.

'Aye,' I said.

I tried to stay cool. I went up the steps, and the clouds over the church roof were just like angels' wings.

Twenty

'You're gonna do *what* with *who*?' said Geordie.

'It's just a walk, man, Geordie.'

'Just a walk? What about what we were going to do?'

'What *were* we going to do?'

'What we always do.'

'What's that, then?'

'How do I know? Hang about and that.'

'Geordie, man. We're not joined at the bliddy hip.'

'You can say that again.' He yanked his cotta off. 'For a *walk*?'

We were in the sacristy, the room in the church where we got changed. There was a massive crucifix, a cabinet for the altar wine and communion hosts, massive drawers and wardrobes for the priests' vestments, racks of candles, boxes of incense, heaps of prayer books, hymn books, pictures of saints with gammy legs and with arrows in them, portraits of dead priests and bishops. There was an altar boys' rota pinned to the wall.

I pulled my white cotta over my head. I undid the buttons on my red cassock and took it off.

'You could come and all,' I said.

'Oh, aye? And play little goosegog Geordie?'

I scratched at the grass stains on my jeans and the dried mud on my shoes. I hung the cassock and cotta in my place on the altar boys' rail. Geordie did the same. He wouldn't look at me.

'There's her mate,' I said.

'The gargoyle, you mean?'

'Geordie, man.'

'I'll go and see the lads up Windy Nook. Mebbes we'll go and ploat some Springwellers.' He pursed his lips and made his voice go girly. 'You go for your nice little walk with your nice little lass.' He headed out of the sacristy. 'Just don't go out walking on Tuesday,' he said. And he went into the church and out of the church and the massive door thudded shut behind him.

I followed him out. I passed Father O'Mahoney coming back in.

'Thank you, Davie,' he said. 'You and your pal did very well.'

He winked.

'Ten bob!' he said.

I went out of the shadowy church into the brilliant light. I hesitated at the top of the church steps. I looked down across Felling to the river. It glistened in the light. It snaked eastwards towards the horizon, the dead flat sea.

I breathed deep and calmed myself and went down to Maria. We were shy with each other. When we started walking we were stiff. We hardly swung our arms in case we knocked against each other. We didn't know what to say. We headed along Sunderland Road and up into Holly Hill Park. It was neat like always: flowers in neat clumps and rows, the lawns and hedges all trimmed, the shrubs pruned, the soil all raked. We passed close to the bowling green. We saw people dressed all in white through gaps in the hedges, saw the rectangle of perfect green, heard little clacks as the bowls struck each other, little bursts of laughter and applause. There was a storm of birdsong from the shrubs and tall trees all around. The parkie saw us. His calliper clicked as he limped towards us. He said nowt, but he narrowed his eyes and raised a finger at us in warning.

'It's all right,' I said to him. 'We'll not cause no bother, Mr Pew.'

He showed us a little black book and mimed writing in it. He made a fist and shook it at us. Then he turned and limped away.

'Does he *ever* talk?' said Maria.

'Just when he yells,' I said. And I imitated him. 'I've got me beady eye on you, boyo! Sling your hook, kidder!'

We walked on, out of the park and on to Holly Hill. We passed the Columba Club. Blurry people were drinking beyond the frosted glass. We laughed again about the horse that was a lion. She said that sometimes she felt closer to animals than she did to people. To grown-up people, anyway.

'I don't want to grow up,' she said. 'Not to be like most people here, anyway. You know what I mean?'

I shrugged.

'They're so tame,' she said. 'They've got such pathetic little lives.'

'Aye,' I said.

'I used to want to be a nun. Thought it might be a way of being special and getting out of here. Then I found out about poverty, chastity, obedience and silence and I thought mebbe it's not for me.'

'I wanted to be a monk. When that White Father came and talked to us.'

'Him! He was gorgeous!'

We walked on. Sometimes our hands brushed gently against each other's. We headed up Split Crow Road towards Watermill Lane where the wide verges were and young trees lined the street. We kept passing neighbours and relatives. They kept calling to us and we waved and called back. They nudged each other, laughed and smiled.

'Look to them all,' Maria said. 'It's like there's never anywhere to get *away*. Hello, Aunty Claire!' she yelled as some woman hurried past with a bag full of shopping.

We walked on.

'You know that Stephen Rose, don't you?' she said.

'Aye.'

'He went away, didn't he?'

'Aye.'

'There's tales about him, aren't there? Are they true?'

'Dunno.'

'People are full of blather, aren't they?'

'Aye,' I said.

'Is he friendly?'

'No.'

'Is he weird?'

'Aye.'

'Nice weird or creepy weird?'

I thought about it.

'Both,' I said.

We walked on. We approached Braddock's Garden. We looked across at Crazy Mary's house. I let my hand touch Maria's hand. I looked into the sky. So blue. The clouds so dazzling white. I tipped my head back and narrowed my eyes.

'What you *doing*?' said Maria.

'Do you think you could think that clouds were angels?' I said.

'You could think anything was anything,' she said. 'It's how your mind works. Prat's a prat but he's right. We could imagine just about anything.'

We walked on. We came to the ancient iron gate. It was rusted, twisted. The lock on it had been ruined years ago.

Maria narrowed her eyes and stared into the sky like me.

'Just look at them all!' she gasped.

Twenty-One

'This is where you go with that Geordie Craggs,' she said. She laughed. 'It's your secret place.'

'How d'you know that?'

She widened her eyes and wobbled her hands.

'Me and Frances Malone know everything! Let's go in.'

I didn't move. I hadn't been in since Stephen and the knife. But now the truce was on, and anyway, Maria was already through the gate and on her way. She ducked through the hawthorn, was disentangling her hair.

'Howay, Davie,' she said.

Going in with a girl was different. I smelled the rot and the piss and the oniony smell in the undergrowth. I felt the mud under my feet and the thorns of the wild roses and brambles on my legs. It felt warm and humid after the breezy street, like the year was further on in here. Sluggish flies buzzed around us. There was years of graffiti on the quarry walls. She said her dad used to come here for soil and daffodil bulbs. Like everybody's dad, I said. Mebbe all the gardens in Felling had bits of this garden in them, I said. Everything was coming into leaf. Blossom was breaking out. There were primroses and fading daffodils and fancier flowers that must have grown from ancient Braddock's seeds. We came through to the clay pond and stood beside it and looked around and I knew what Maria meant when she said it was beautiful.

'There's talk they're going to fill it in,' she said. 'They're going to bulldoze the gardens and knock the last of the old house down and fill the quarry in and build a new estate.'

'I heard,' I said.

'They're cretins,' she said. 'They'll call the new streets Pretty Place and Lovely Lane but they'll not see how they've smashed a bit of Paradise.'

She looked into the sky.

'Stop them doing it!' she called.

We stepped around the pond. The pale mud squirmed under our feet. She slipped and I grabbed her hand till she was steady. The fire smouldered outside the cave. We went to the entrance and I caught my breath at what we saw in there.

There were clay figures everywhere. Little goblins sat in niches in the rock. There were little pigs and dragons. There were lumpy unfinished things leaning on the walls. They were all blackened, covered in ash. Maria knelt down and touched a twisted little man.

'He makes them in the fire,' I said.

'Who does?'

'Stephen Rose.'

I kicked at the embers. A curled-up clay body lay in there.

'I saw his apostles,' she said. 'They were beautiful. These are all ugly, but they're still beautiful.'

I scanned the cave again. Geordie would be furious. Mouldy and Skinner and Poke would just smash up everything. Then I saw the sign painted in white on the cave roof. The silly warnings from Mouldy's lot and from us had been painted out. There was just a single message.

Anything that is destroyed will be avenged. S.R.

'Really weird,' said Maria.

'He's had a weird life.'

'There but for the grace of God,' she said, like everyone in Felling seemed to say. She crossed herself. We sat close to each other on a pair of stones. I held her hand again and she didn't take it away. The quarry was filled with noises, clicks and buzzings and breezes. There were noises that must have been animals moving in the undergrowth. Birds sang. Something snorted not too far away. It came closer, stopped, moved away again.

'Do you believe in power?' I said.

'What do you mean, power?'

'Dunno. Power. Like the power to do things nobody else could do.'

'Magic, you mean?'

'Something like that. Do you believe somebody could make something and make it live?'

She looked into the sky. She narrowed her eyes.

'That's what women do,' she said. 'Make living babies that come out of them and crawl and cry.'

'Aye, there's that,' I said. 'Flesh and blood. But could you make something that isn't flesh and blood? Could you make something out of clay, and make *that* live?'

We looked down at the fire. A hip was visible among the fading embers, a foot, the angle of an elbow.

'They say all kinds of things can happen in the world,' she said. 'You hear all kinds of stories.'

'Aye.'

'Like that baby.'

'What baby?'

'The one that was born at the Queen Elizabeth. It was all hairy. It had paws where the hands should be. Did you not hear?'

I shook my head.

'Frances' mam knows somebody that used to be a nurse there. She saw it. She said it was half-dog, half-human.'

'Half-dog?'

'Aye. It stayed alive for a bit, then it died.'

'How could that happen?'

We shook our heads at each other.

'They say it came out of a Stoneygate lass,' she whispered.

'No.'

'Aye. And they say that the lass has been out of her senses ever since. And they say there's been stranger things than that. Things that's never known except to the doctors. Deformities. Freaks of nature. Things there seems no reason for. Things that seem impossible.'

She stroked the backs of her hands, her shoulders, her cheeks.

'We should be glad to be just as we are,' she said. 'There but . . .'

'They say that one day we'll be able to make life in test tubes,' I said. 'We'll be able to create living creatures with chemicals and electricity and nuclear power.'

'Trouble with that is,' she said, 'mebbe we won't know where to stop.'

'And we'll make monsters.'

'Aye. And mebbe the monsters'll turn on us, and threaten us, and be the end of us.'

I looked down at the creature in the embers.

'All this is what you asked Prat about, isn't it?' she said.

'Aye.'

She leaned forward and turned her face so she could look right at me.

'Is it because *you've* got some kind of power?' she said.

'Me? Don't be daft.'

We were silent then. The snorting thing moved away from us. A dog, I thought. A hedgehog. Maria heard it. She looked at me.

'A hedgehog,' I said.

She nodded.

Hundreds of tadpoles were swimming in the pale water. Already lots of them had lost their tails and were growing legs. Maria stirred the water with a stick and giggled at the way the tadpoles twisted and turned and flickered around it.

'There's dead dogs in here,' she said.

'So they say. And dead cats.'

'And sacks of puppies and kittens.'

'It's what the tadpoles live on.'

'And the fish and the beetles.'

'Dead things,' she whispered.

'Death.'

She stirred more quickly and the water swirled and splashed, and as we watched, a frog swam up from the murky depths.

'Oh, look!' she said.

'We called him out,' I said.

'Hello, Mr Frog,' she said.

She giggled.

'Look at him,' she said. 'What a funny thing. Just an ordinary frog! Even the ordinary things can seem dead weird, can't they?'

I watched it swim to the edge and perch on a stone and it glistened in the sunlight.

'Aye,' I said. 'Dead weird.'

We could see the throb in its throat, the throb of its heart. It seemed so peaceful sitting there, so ugly, so lovely, so strange.

'Look, ickle tadpoles!' she said. 'There's your big daddy.'

Then the grass snake came. It darted out of the darkness of the undergrowth. It took the frog in its jaws. It bit and crushed and gripped. The frog struggled and kicked but there was nothing it could do. The snake started to swallow the frog head first. It was over in minutes. The snake closed its jaws. The frog was just a great lump in the snake's body. The snake was dead still for a while, then it slithered sluggishly back to where it had come from.

'Oh,' breathed Maria. 'Oh, my God.'

Our hands were clenched tight together. We goggled into each other's eyes.

'That was . . .' I said.

'Astonishing,' she said.

We shuddered. We looked at the dark surrounding undergrowth, at the quarry's dark rim, at the silent still figures around us in the cave.

'I think we should go,' whispered Maria.

We edged around the pond. High above, the clouds were turning red. I narrowed my eyes. The angels you could imagine up there were thinner darker things now. We stumbled away from the quarry towards the entrance. We heard snorting behind us. We looked back. Nothing. We laughed. But we moved more quickly. The snorting came closer. There was the noise of undergrowth being pushed aside as something hurried through it. We laughed again, but we started running, hand in hand. We ducked through the thorn trees. The thorns caught our hair, caught our clothes. We pushed through the gate on to Watermill Lane. Out on the breezy street again, we giggled. We looked back. Nothing there.

'Silly us,' said Maria.

We kissed each other. We held each other tight and pressed our lips together hard. She grunted as we stepped apart.

'Look.'

I turned. Stephen was at Crazy Mary's front door, watching us.

'Creepy weird,' she whispered.

He came towards us.

'Hello, Davie,' he said.

He looked past us into the garden.

'What was after you?' he said. His eyes widened. 'Get back!' he yelled. 'Get back, I tell you!'

We looked behind, but there was nothing there, of course.

'Just nowt at all,' said Stephen. He smiled. 'You were deceived.'

Then he looked at Maria.

'Who's this?' he said.

'Me name's Maria if you must know,' said Maria.

She turned away. He caught my arm and held me back and breathed his words into my ear.

'I know what I need you for. There's a purpose for you, Davie.'

I tried to pull away.

'Don't bother with the lass,' he said.

He passed his hand before my eyes.

'Oh, look!' he said.

He pointed. I saw Mouldy further down the street, watching.

'It's OK,' said Stephen. 'He won't come. Not now.'

He suddenly kissed my cheek.

'What you doing?' I said.

I pulled away. He started laughing.

I had to hurry to get to Maria's side. She slowed down. We looked back and watched Stephen going in, closing Crazy's door behind him. And we saw Mouldy turning a corner, disappearing.

'Very very creepy weird,' she said. She regarded me. 'What's between you two?'

'What do you mean? Nowt's between us.'

She looked back. She regarded me.

'Lads is strange,' she said.

I tried to shift from her gaze. Her eyes widened.

'It's coming!' she said.

I spun around to look. Nothing there. We giggled.

I tried to kiss her again, but she stepped back.

'Silly you,' she said. 'Silly us.'

Twenty-Two

We met on neutral ground, at dusk. We used the graveyard at Heworth. We stood in the oldest part, where the ancient weathered graves were. There were thin tall trees around us. There were clusters of black nests in the branches. Our grave was a table-high and blackened thing. Skinner and Poke were on one side, Geordie and me on the other. The sky had lost its brightness, blue had turned to grey.

'Where is he?' said Geordie.

Skinner shrugged.

'Probly in The Swan. We telt him seven o'clock. It's not far past.'

'You're sure he's OK about the truce?' said Geordie.

'That's what he said,' answered Skinner. 'You telling me you don't believe him?'

He laughed and rolled his sleeve back and showed his wound, a thin scar on his forearm.

'It'll be marked for ever,' he said.

He looked at us, dead cold.

'Your mate's a maniac,' he said.

'He's not our mate,' said Geordie.

'No?' said Skinner.

He was a little wiry kid with knuckles hard as stone. In one of our fights, he'd nutted Geordie and Geordie still had the scar on his nose from it. But he was the one that started pulling Mouldy off me that time. He was the one that yelled, 'Don't! You'll kill him, man!' And he'd quickly checked my throat and my face before he laughed and ran away.

We waited. I ran my fingers across the names of the people buried below. There was a whole bunch of the Braddocks, all of them dead for a hundred years or more. The stone said they had entered unto glory. I thought of them crumbling away, flesh and blood and bones turning to slime, turning to dust. By now there was probably nothing to separate them from earth, from soil, from clay. I looked towards the graves where we'd buried the two blokes just a few days back. What were those blokes like now? How close to dust were they?

'Mebbe we got the times mixed up,' I found myself saying. 'Mebbe we should just abandon it.'

Poke grinned.

'Scared?' he said.

I shook my head. One day months back, I'd fought with him. We'd battled till we were both worn out. Nobody won. I ached for days. The grazes and bruises took an age to go away. 'What's the point of it?' my mam said when she saw all the marks on me. But Dad said not to worry. It was just the way things were. He shook his head. 'Lads,' he said.

It got darker. We waited. Then Skinner whispered, 'Look!'

And there was Mouldy, lumbering through the graves.

'Mouldy!' called Skinner. 'We're over here!'

Mouldy came to the head of the grave.

'Hiya, Mouldy,' said Poke.

Mouldy glanced at him, curled his lip. He wiped a fist across his face, lit a cigarette. His eyes settled on me. They were empty, dead.

'So?' he grunted.

No one spoke. He thumped the grave with his fist.

'So?' he said.

'The kid with the knife's not our mate,' said Geordie.

Mouldy licked a knuckle. I saw him as he would be in five years' time, sluggish, heavy, slow, a great gut on him, a drunken dope that nobody'd take notice of. He pointed at me.

'He's his mate. I seen him, talking to him.'

'Aye,' said Geordie. 'But—'

Mouldy thumped the grave again.

'Shuddup! I seen him. And I seen lovey-dovey stuff and whispering stuff.'

'Lovey-dovey?' said Skinner.

'I seen the new sod kissing this sod.'

'Kissing?' said Skinner.

'Aye. There was a bint there. She seen it and all.' Mouldy kept his eyes on me. 'Say I'm a liar,' he said.

I said nothing. He shaped a fist, pretended to go for me, grinned again when Poke caught his arm.

'It's a truce, Mouldy,' said Skinner.

'Liars cannot make truces,' said Mouldy. He shaped his fist again. 'You're a lying Catholic Felling bastard,' he said. He blinked. He looked at each of us in turn. 'What you going to say to that?' he said.

None of us spoke. High above, beyond the trees, above the church, great streaks of red had appeared in the sky.

'OK, then,' Mouldy said. 'I'll do the lying bastard now.'

'Don't,' I whispered.

I backed away from the grave.

'Geordie,' I said.

'There's a truce,' said Geordie, but Mouldy just spat at him, a gobful straight into his face.

I ran. Mouldy came after me. He kicked my feet away. I crashed to the ground. He stamped on my head and my ribs and my back. Everything was black and starry till the others were pulling him away. I curled up against a gravestone. *For they are like unto the angels*, it said.

'Davie, run!' said Geordie.

'Run!' said Skinner.

And I picked myself up and belted out of the graveyard and on to Watermill Lane and kept running till I saw the dark figure waiting. Stephen Rose, leaning against a tree. I slowed, stopped.

'Davie,' he said.

I looked behind. Nothing.

'It's all right, Davie. There's nowt there.'

His voice softened.

'Relax, Davie.'

Twenty-Three

Home was a hundred yards away. Lights burned in the windows. I wanted Dad to come out, or Mam. I wanted them to yell out into the street and send Stephen running back to Crazy Mary's. But they didn't come out. Nothing moved. The darkness deepened. Stephen breathed his calming words. He passed his hand before my eyes. And I did relax. And I thought of the angel that had cast Stephen down and raised him up, and I thought of the power that I had seen flowing from him and I told myself that Stephen Rose was something strange and new, something that had been sent to me, something that stood before me as I grew from being a boy into a man. I couldn't turn away. So I said to him,

'What you after, Stephen?'

He shrugged.

'Just a word or two.'

I looked towards the Sacred Heart medallion

silhouetted in our door. *Deliver me from evil*, I said inside.

He touched the weal on my cheek.

'Mouldy done it?' he said.

'Aye.'

'He'd be better off dead, eh?'

I didn't answer. He laughed softly.

'He would,' he said. 'We all know that. Just imagine. No Mouldy. No monster.'

'He'll be a slob soon enough,' I said. 'Just got to keep out of his way till then.'

He laughed.

'You're not doing very well so far.'

I laughed with him.

'Just imagine if it happened, Davie. Just imagine you're fast asleep in bed and you wake up and it's a sunny ordinary morning and your mam says to you, "Did you hear that Martin Mould is dead?" '

He grinned.

'It'd be something to celebrate, eh? Martin Mould is dead! Go on, admit it. Aye?'

I shrugged.

'Aye,' I said.

'Good. Now listen. My angel come again.'

'Your angel?'

'The one I telt you about. You've never forgotten

her? Anyway, she talked about you. She telt me you could help me in me work.'

'An *angel*? Stephen, man. It's just barmy.'

'I know. It's mental, it's barmy, but it's true. And isn't it what they tell you in church? We are not alone. There's precious beings all around us. So why should you be surprised?'

I looked up past the streetlights towards the stars.

'It's still bliddy crazy,' I said.

'I know,' he said. 'But mebbe the craziest things is the truest things of all.'

He grinned while I thought about his words.

'Look,' he said. 'Here's a really crazy thing.'

He reached down into the grass verge at the pavement's side. He ripped the turf open and tugged out a handful of soil. He spat into it. He spat again. He held it in the pale pool of light cast by a streetlight.

'You as well,' he told me. 'Spit into me hand. So a bit of you is in it. Do it, man.'

I spat into the soil. He worked it with his fingers. He spat again, told me to spit again. I spat again. The soil was damp and pliable. He rolled it on his palm: a fat wormy thing, a sluggy thing. He raised it to his lips.

'Move,' he whispered. 'Live.'

He held it on his opened palm.

'Tell it, Davie,' he whispered. He raised his eyes to

me. 'You got to,' he said. 'Gan on. Tell it to move. Tell it to live.'

I felt so stupid. I couldn't speak, then the words came out.

'Move . . . Live . . . Move . . . Live . . .'

'Be tough, Davie,' said Stephen. 'Command it.'

He passed his hand before my eyes.

I spoke again.

'Move. Live.'

And the thing moved. It squirmed on Stephen's palm in the silvery light. It squirmed like there was life in it, like there was spirit in it.

'See?' he whispered while we watched in wonder. 'The power is in you, Davie, just like it is in me.'

And we watched the squirming thing a moment longer then he let it fall back to the earth. He wiped the dirt from his hands.

'Really crazy,' he said. 'Really true. Do you agree? Do you believe?'

I shook my head. How could I *not* believe?

'Yes,' I said. 'But how can we do it?'

'That was just a little bit of easy magic. We can do lots more together. Lots more true and crazy things. That's what the angel was on about.'

'What did she say?'

'She said that my strength and your strength isn't

enough. She said we'll also need the strength of the Lord to help us.'

I met his eye.

'The strength of the Lord?' I said. 'How the Hell do we get that?'

'You get it for us, Davie. You get the body and blood of Christ and bring it back here. It's your task.'

He smiled.

'You're the good altar boy, Davie. You got to steal the body and blood of Christ.'

'An angel telt you to tell me to do *that*?'

He shrugged. He looked at me dead calm, like he was daring me to believe him.

'Aye,' he said. 'She did. Angels work in mysterious ways, Davie.'

'And what good will it do?'

'It'll help us make a . . .'

'A what?'

He studied the sky, the thickening stars.

'A creature, Davie. A thing that will stand up and walk beside us and protect us.' He laughed. 'A monster!' He breathed the words into my ear. 'A bliddy monster. A thing that'll terrify Mouldy and brutes like Mouldy. A thing that'll even kill him for us, if that's what we tell it to do.'

I glanced at the house.

'Come out,' I said inside myself. 'Get me away from this.'

'When's your next Mass?' said Stephen.

I searched my memory.

'Sunday,' I said.

'You got to do it then.'

He slid something cold and metallic into my hand.

'Put them in this,' he said, 'and keep them safe.'

It was a small round silver locket.

'Will you do it?' he said.

He looked into the sky.

'They are,' he said. 'The precious beings is looking down on us. Mebbe one day they'll show themselves to you and all, Davie. Will you do it?'

I laughed. I laughed at Stephen, at me, at dreams of monsters and angels and illusions of moving clay. Stupid, all of it. Crazy.

'Will you, Davie?' he said.

'Why not? Yes.'

'Good,' he said. 'They'll be very pleased with you.'

Then Mam's voice came.

'Davie?'

She was coming out of the front door. She was standing at our garden gate. She was coming down the pavement to me.

'Davie? What you doing, Davie?'

I rubbed my eyes.

'It was just Stephen,' I said.

'Stephen?'

'Stephen Rose.' I looked around. Stephen was gone. 'I was just talking to him.'

'When, Davie? There's nobody here.'

I looked around again.

'Davie! What's up with you, son?'

'Nowt,' I said.

'There's nobody here,' she said. 'I saw nobody at all.'

Twenty-Four

Inside the house, she touched the wound on my cheek.

'What's this?'

I looked down.

'Fighting again!' she said.

I tried to shake my head.

'Fighting *again*,' she said.

She stared into my eyes.

'It'll end in something *awful*,' she said.

She shook me again.

'Snap out of it, will you?' She chewed her lips, she peered into my eyes. 'What's been happening? You're in a dream. You're scared stiff.'

'No, I'm not.'

'Yes, you *are*. And talking in the street to somebody that isn't there . . .'

'Yes, he *was*.'

'Not to my eyes he wasn't.'

'He must have run away. You must have missed him.'

'And who hit you? And how hard?'

She was nearly in tears.

'Nobody,' I said. 'It's nowt, Mam.'

I tried to pull away but she wouldn't let me go.

'*Nowt?*'

'Nowt.'

She gave me some aspirin and some tea. She opened a bottle of Lourdes water and dabbed my head with it.

'I'm taking you to the doctor,' she said.

'*No.*'

'Do you feel dizzy? Do you feel sick?'

'*No!*'

She watched me.

'It's got to stop,' she said.

'It will.'

'When?'

'Now.'

'You promise? You *promise*?'

'Yes!'

She turned away. I drank my tea. Soon Dad came home. She told him about it.

'Who was it?' he said.

He knew I wouldn't tell him.

'Whoever it is,' he said, 'this has to be an end to it.'

He put his arm around me. He turned me away from Mam.

'It must stop. Things like this can escalate, get out of hand. This is how bloody wars start, man . . .'

'I know that, Dad.'

'Promise me you'll put an end to it.'

I said nothing.

'Promise me, Davie.'

'I promise.'

All evening they watched me. Mam kept asking,

'Do you feel dizzy? Do you feel sick?'

'No.' I kept answering. '*No.*'

'I'll put an end to it,' I lied.

'I promise,' I lied.

Twenty-Five

I stole the body and blood of Christ at Mass that Sunday. I knelt below the priest on the altar. He had the round Communion bread in his hands. He murmured the magic words,

'This is my body.'

He held the chalice of wine and murmured,

'This is my blood.'

The congregation bowed their heads, closed their eyes, beat their breasts.

The bread still looked like bread. The wine still looked like wine. But a miracle had happened. They'd turned into the body and blood of Christ. Christ himself was with us on the altar.

The priest ate the body and drank the blood.

Geordie and I opened our mouths and stuck out our tongues to receive our own Communion bread.

Then the congregation left their seats and headed for

the altar rail. Maria was there, and Frances, and my mam and dad, and Crazy Mary, and loads of our family, friends, neighbours. They queued in the aisles. They knelt at the altar rail. They lowered their eyes and prayed and waited. I got my little silver tray and went down with Father O'Mahoney to them. They closed their eyes, stuck their tongues out. The priest pressed a Communion wafer on to every tongue. 'The body of Christ,' he murmured. 'Amen,' they said.

I held the tray below each face, to catch the falling crumbs. They fell like tiny grains of dust. They fell and danced through shafts of sunlight pouring from the high narrow windows of the church. They lay there on the gleaming silver tray. A tiny fragment fell as Father O'Mahoney gave the bread to Crazy Mary. Another fell below the lips of Noreen Craggs. We moved from upturned face to upturned face. The voices murmured, the faces shone, the dust and fragments fell. Then it was done, and the last of the communicants went back to the seats.

I followed the priest up the altar steps. I tilted the tray, I quickly took a pinch of the fragments and dust. I pressed it into the strip of Sellotape in my cassock pocket. I quickly took another pinch. At the altar, I handed the tray to the priest. He ran his own finger round the tray, and licked away the fragments of Christ's body. He did it again till none was left. Then he slurped the last of the wine. He wiped the inside of the chalice with a pure white linen cloth and put it on the altar.

He said the final prayers. He told the congregation to go in peace, the Mass was over. Thanks be to God, they said.

Twenty-Six

I nicked the wine-stained cloth in the sacristy as Father O'Mahoney was taking his vestments off. I swapped it with a clean cloth from a drawer. Father O'Mahoney put this into a little basket of things that would be taken away to be washed by nuns. I stuffed the cloth and the Sellotape into my jeans pocket. Geordie saw me. He looked at me. I glared at him.

Father O'Mahoney stretched and sighed.

'What a grand morning it is, lads!' he said. 'Did you see those great shafts of sunlight blazing through the church?'

'Aye, Father,' we said.

He took an imaginary golf club in his hands. He mimed swinging at a golf ball.

'Oh, to be in Kerry on a day like this!' he said.

He looked into the far distance, indicated a huge imaginary landscape with his hands.

'The mountains, the beaches, the ocean, Dingle and the Blasket Islands and the Skellig Rocks, the call of the curlews and the sound of the surf . . . You should see it, boys! Ireland! The ball flies straighter there, and oh so true, and the greens are truly green and the ball drops down into the hole with a lovely little . . . plop! It's God's own land, that's what it is.'

He grinned.

'But that's enough of that. The little course at Windy Nook's a grand substitute.' He rubbed his hands in excitement. 'So. What shenanigans have you two planned for today?'

Geordie shrugged. I said nowt. Father O'Mahoney grinned again.

'Getting too old to share it now?' he said. He winked. 'Specially when the girls might be involved.'

He put his arms around our shoulders.

'You're a good pair. Always were. Now go on. Off to your adventures. And I'll get looking for those clubs of mine.'

As we left, he called after us:

'You know, boys, I often think we're already living in the borderlands of Paradise! Good day to you now!'

Outside the church, Geordie said,

'What you doing with the cloth?'

144

'Nowt,' I said.

I tried to move away from him.

'What's up with you?' he said.

'Nowt,' I said.

'You're always nicking off,' he said.

'No, I'm not,' I said.

'Yes, you bliddy are. It'll be that lass again.'

'Don't be daft.'

'Who you calling daft?'

'Nobody. You.'

'That's right.'

'What do you mean, that's right? You mean it's true you're daft?'

'I must be, hanging out with you.'

'Nick off, then.'

'I will. And you nick off and all.'

'I will.'

So we both nicked off. I ran up the High Street, across the square. I came to a halt. I stared at myself in The Blue Bell's window. There I was, an ordinary kid. This was home, an ordinary town. I'd stolen the body and blood of Christ and I wouldn't give them back. I'd go further into the darkness with Stephen Rose. I'd make a monster if I could. I moved closer to the window, I looked at myself more closely. I was just the same as ever, ordinary, just ordinary.

'Is this what going crazy's like?' I whispered. 'Is this what being under a spell is like?'

Then I tore myself away and ran again.

Twenty-Seven

I inspected the Sellotape in my bedroom. The dust and fragments of Christ's body were still stuck to it. I folded it and put it into the locket. I cut out the little wine-stained pieces of the altar cloth. I put them into the locket as well. I looked at what I had. A few shreds. Next to nowt. How could there be a power in things like this? I stared hard at them, willing them to do something marvellous.

'Do something,' I whispered.

They did nowt. My heart sank.

'What the Hell you doing, man?' I said to myself.

I snapped the locket shut.

The sun blazed into my bedroom. A crystal clear sky, nothing in it but a few small birds nearby and the sparrowhawk that spiralled over Braddock's Garden. Lunch was on downstairs: the lovely scents of beef and vegetables and a boiling pudding. Somebody yelled jokes on the radio. Dad roared with laughter. Mam sang along with the radio's daft songs. She yelled that the food'd be on the table in five minutes. I sat there on my bed. Said some prayers. Prayed for forgiveness. Slid the locket right under my mattress. Prayed again. Knew there might be no forgiveness for what I'd done.

'Davie!' yelled Mam. 'DAVIE!'

I went down.

Everything was dried out and tasteless.

Mam kept asking if I was all right.

'Aye,' I told her.

She reached out to touch me.

'I'm all right, man!' I snapped.

She flinched.

Dad's eyes narrowed and he raised his finger at me.

'That's enough of that, lad,' he said.

He shook his head. We ate in silence. I stuffed a lump of suet pudding into my mouth.

'Lads,' he muttered.

Afterwards we put the TV on and an ancient black-and-white film of Frankenstein came on. We watched the monster lumbering about. Mam laughed at how clumsy it all was.

'Remember when we saw it first?' she said to Dad. 'All them folk in the Corona fainting and screaming and running out? What on earth were we so terrified of?'

Dad lurched about the room for a bit with his arms stretched out and his legs dead stiff and he grunted and groaned and pretended to attack us.

Then Maria and Frances walked past and Frances stared in at the window.

'Aha!' said Mam.

'You'll be off out now, I suppose?' said Dad.

'No,' I said.

Maria waved. I ignored her, turned my face back to the TV. From the corner of my eye I saw her link her arm into Frances' and lead her away.

'You're sure?' said Mam.

The monster growled.

'Aye,' I snapped. 'Aye, man!'

'Davie!' said Dad. 'That's enough!'

'Stop me then!' I said. 'Go on, bliddy stop me!'

He dropped his act, glared at me.

'Get to your damn room,' he said.

I rushed upstairs, back to the body, the blood, the fear. I sat all afternoon. I climbed into the cupboard in my wall. I clambered over toys and games to find my earliest things: rattles and building blocks and crayons and board books and found my ancient tub of Plasticine. All the colours had blended to earthy grey. The stuff felt hard as stone but as my fingers worked it softened. I remembered making animals, fish, birds, little models of my beloved mam and dad. I made a beast and whispered time and again and time and again, 'Live and move. Live and move!' I made a little model of myself and hated it and turned it to a four-legged stupid thing with a heavy head hanging down towards the floor. 'Live and move,' I told it. 'Live and move.' As dusk came on, the air outside seemed filled with angels that hovered over the streetlights and peered in at me with disappointed, disapproving faces.

There was a knock at the door and Mam slipped in. She held a piece of chocolate out to me.

She smiled.

'Plasticine!' she said. 'Remember how you used to love it?'

'No,' I said. 'Well, kind of.'

She smelled a little piece of it.

'Takes me back. Remember when there were little creatures everywhere?'

'Dunno,' I said.

'You'll have forgotten. Would you like to come downstairs?'

'Dunno.'

She put an arm around me.

'I'm sorry, Mam,' I said.

'Is it something to do with a girl?'

'No. Dunno, Mam.'

'Or is it Geordie mebbe?'

'Geordie!'

She laughed gently. She gave me more chocolate.

'Whatever it is, it's not nice when somebody you love turns on you like that,' she said.

'Aye. I know. I'm—'

She pressed a finger to my lips.

'That's OK. Say sorry to your dad as well and that'll be an end to it.'

I did go down again and apologise to Dad, and he too said that was an end to it but nothing stopped. I spent that night awake, making Plasticine creatures, breathing prayers and incantations and commands on them while the moon shone down at me. I didn't dare to open the locket and try to use the power of the body and the blood. Nothing moved, till four a.m. 'Please move,' I whispered, and a fragment of the Plasticine did seem to come to a kind of life, did seem to slither on my palm, but by then I was fighting sleep, I was probably dreaming, or it was just another sign that I was going mad.

Twenty-Eight

'She'll chuck you,' said Frances.

She walked into me in the corridor. We were on our way to Prat's class. It was Friday, last lesson of the day.

'Who will?'

'Marilyn Monroe. Who do you think? You saw us, didn't you?'

I shrugged.

'You saw us and took not a blind bit of bliddy notice,' she said. 'Why should she want a lad that ignores her then walks round in a dream all day?'

'Dunno.'

'Dunno. That says it all.'

She poked me in the ribs.

'What's wrong with you? Can you not see how lovely she is? What's going on in that stupid skull of yours?'

I was going to say Dunno but I didn't.

She clicked her fingers in front of my face.

'Hello,' she said. 'Hello-o. Is anybody there?'

I shrugged.

She shook her head.

'That's it,' she said. 'I'll tell her today. Chuck him, I'll say.'

'Let her chuck me!'

'She will. You're a waste of bliddy time.'

She hurried on. Maria was already in the class. By the time I got in, Frances was hissing in Maria's ear and waggling her hands about. They both started giggling. They looked straight at me then turned away and made faces and hooted. I sat down beside Geordie. He slid his chair away from me.

'Settle down!' said Prat.

He looked at some notes.

'Where was I?' he said.

'Up your bum,' said Geordie.

'Aha!' said Prat. 'Clay!'

He held up a little sphere of it between his fingers.

'The basest thing of all,' he said. 'A lump of muck. Soft, oozy, slimy, slithery, formless stuff. Could it be that we are drawn to it because it reminds us of ourselves – of our own human formlessness and muckiness?'

He paused. He looked around the room.

'Muckiness,' he said. 'Is it true? Can we use such a word about ourselves?'

Nobody answered.

Frances turned her eyes to me. She nodded.

'You're saying yes?' said Prat.

'Oh, yes, sir,' said Frances.

'And yet there are some,' continued Prat, 'who say that we are the opposite of muck, that we are blessed spirits. Is that true? Who thinks that? Who thinks' – he lowered his voice – 'that we are like angels?'

Geordie raised his hand.

'Me, sir,' he said.

'Thank you, George,' said Prat. 'I've often thought that about you myself. *But . . .*' He widened his eyes. He raised a finger, like he always did when he thought he was getting dead profound. 'Isn't it true that the truth is somewhere in between? Isn't it true that we are both? We are muck *and* we are spirit! Who agrees with that?'

'Me, sir,' muttered several kids.

'Excellent! Then let's move on. Could it be that we love to work with clay because it shows how the creative act can . . .'

'Bliddy Hell,' muttered Geordie. 'Does he never stop?'

Prat blathered on. He strode back and forward in front of us, closing his eyes, tapping his temples, gazing at the sky outside.

Geordie regarded me. He scribbled something on a piece of paper and slid it across to me.

What was Mouldy on about? Kissing stuff.

'Eh?' I breathed.

He wrote again.

Kissing. Lovey-dovey stuff.

He watched me. There was a grin playing about his face. I clicked my tongue, made a face. He rolled his eyes and puckered his mouth as if to kiss. I started to write something on the note but I didn't know what to write.

Nick off, I scribbled at last.

He pretended to be shocked.

'Are you all right, George?' said Prat in mid-stream.

'Aye, sir.'

'Excellent. For a second I believed that you were in the process of reacting to my words.'

'Oh, no, sir.'

'Excellent.'

Prat flicked his hand up and caught a jelly baby that was flying through the air. He popped it into his mouth.

'Sometimes,' he said, 'I wonder to myself, "Why do I tell them such things? Why do I bother?" '

'Cos you're a prat,' muttered Geordie.

'But I refuse to be downcast. I tell myself, "But there are those who do listen, Peter Patrick Parker, as there always have been and always will." So . . .! Whose are the jelly babies, by the way?'

'Mine, sir,' said Jimmy Kay.

'Then I will have another, James, to feed the stream of words. A red one, please.' Jimmy lobbed one to him, Prat caught it, chewed it, plunged on again. 'Could it be,' he said, 'that in a lump of this clay we see a body without a soul, and it inspires us to . . .'

'Bliddy Hell,' Geordie said again.

Kissing, he wrote. *Davie and Stephen Rose are . . .*

I read it. I curled my lip at him. He scribbled another note, rolled it up, lobbed it towards Frances and Maria. Frances opened it. She clapped her hand across her mouth. She goggled. She giggled.

'Eeee!' she said, and she passed the note on to Maria.

Maria furrowed her brow. She looked across at me. Her eyes were blank, then Frances nudged her and whispered in her ear again and Maria started giggling as well.

Prat blathered on.

'Eeeee!' said Frances.

'Yes, Miss Malone?' said Prat.

'Well, sir,' said Frances. 'It's very . . . er . . .'

'Disturbing?' said Prat.

'Aye, sir,' said Frances.

'Terrifying, even?'

'Aye, sir.'

'Indeed. The thought that we might be doomed simply to return to earth? The thought that we may be dense, solid, heavy, the playthings of our creator . . .'

'It's shocking, sir,' said Frances.

'Indeed,' said Prat.

'Appalling,' said Frances.

She giggled.

'Disgraceful, degrading, disgusting,' she said. 'Maria thinks so as well.'

'Does she?' said Prat.

Frances nudged her.

'Oh, yes, sir,' said Maria.

Prat beamed.

'It is just a notion,' he said. 'An idea.'

He put his hands on to the girls' desk and leaned over them.

'I am so glad that I have made you *think*.'

'Oh, we're certainly thinking, sir,' said Maria.

'Eeee!' said Frances. She rolled her eyes at me. 'Eeee! Eeeeeee!'

Afterwards, in the corridor, I tried to just get away. But the girls giggled behind me in the corridor. Geordie egged them on. So I turned back and glared. Geordie squealed, pretended to be scared.

'Get stuffed,' I said.

158

I tried to catch Maria's eye. I wanted to say to her: 'Look how we were together in the quarry.' I wanted to say to Geordie: 'But you've always been my best mate.' But Maria grinned and wouldn't meet my eye. Geordie simpered. I clenched my fists. Geordie waved me on.

'Howay, then,' he said. 'Try it, Davie.'

I hesitated.

'Howay,' he said. 'What's up? You scared?'

So I went for him and we battled and loads of kids gathered round us and yelled and chanted:

'Fight! Fight! Fight! Fight!'

Geordie thumped me in the gut and winded me but I stood up to it. I swung my fist and caught him in the nose and blood burst out. He squealed and jumped at me. I went for his throat. We sprawled on the ground and we grunted and cried and cursed.

'You bastard!' we kept yelling. 'You bliddy snake!'

Then Prat was running and yelling for it to stop. I got free and stood up. I leaned down over Geordie.

'I hate you!' I snarled.

Then I ran.

Twenty-Nine

I spat on the ground as I left the school. I cursed them all. Mouldy was sitting on a bench outside the graveyard near The Swan. He was drunk, half-asleep, a useless lump. I went closer. He looked at me through glassy eyes. No recognition in them.

'Fishface,' I hissed. I clenched my fists. 'Think I'm scared of you?'

He growled. I leaned towards him.

'Fishface. Fishface.'

He hauled himself forward, tried to stand up, dropped back to the bench again.

'Fishface fatso slob,' I said.

I grinned and walked on. I passed right in front of him. I smelled him and hated him.

'Pig,' I told him. 'Think I'm scared of you?'

I picked a stone up, weighed it in my hand, caught an image of it crashing on to Mouldy's temple, heard him groan, saw him slump and twitch, saw the blood spurt. The temptation passed. I gently dropped the stone again.

I knocked on Crazy Mary's door. Stephen let me in.

'I got the stuff,' I said.

'Good lad!'

He hugged me. I pulled away.

'Show it, then,' he said.

'I've not got it on me, man.'

He took me to the kitchen. Crazy Mary was at the table with a cup of tea in front of her.

'Hello, Miss Doonan,' I said.

No reply. Stephen sniggered.

'Hello, stupid crazy bint,' he said.

Mary sat dead still. No reply.

'We'll do it this weekend,' said Stephen.

He grinned.

'We'll make a monster this weekend, Davie,' he said. 'Tomorrow night. Right?'

He held my face in his hands.

'Right?' he said.

'Right!'

I glanced at Mary. What would she be making of our words?

Stephen giggled.

'Watch!' he said.

He dropped his jeans. He stuck his bare backside towards Mary. She did nothing. He pulled his jeans up.

'Have a go!' he said. 'Go on! Drop your trousers and do it as well.'

He laughed in my face.

'It's just a trick, man. Watch.'

He stretched his hand to Mary's face. He clicked his fingers.

'Five, four, three, two, one,' he said. 'Wake up, Mary.'

Crazy Mary blinked and twitched.

'Look,' said Stephen. 'Somebody's come calling on us, Aunty Mary.'

She looked at me.

'It's me pal, Davie,' said Stephen.

Mary smiled.

'It's the good altar boy,' she said. 'The lad with the lovely mam. Would you like some jam and bread, pet?' She shook her head. 'Didn't hear nobody come in, though.'

'You dropped off, Aunty Mary,' said Stephen.

'Aye,' she said. 'I must of.'

She stared at her nephew, then at me.

'D'you think God protects us when we're fast asleep?' she said.

'Course he does,' said Stephen. 'He looks down on each and every one of us and keeps us safe. That's his job.'

'Me boy's such a comfort to me,' said Mary.

She got a knife and started sawing at a loaf of bread. She cut a couple of slices. She held them up to Heaven.

'Everything on this earth is thine,' she said.

Stephen groaned.

'Ballocks,' he said. 'Time to put her down again. Aunty Mary.' She turned. He passed his hand before her eyes.

'Put the bread down,' he said.

She put it down.

'Sit down.'

She sat down.

'You will sleep now, Mary,' he said. 'You will wake only when I tell you to.'

Her eyes stayed open, but the light disappeared from them.

Stephen grinned.

'Just a trick,' he said. 'Some's much more susceptible than others. She's a piece of cake.'

He watched me.

'I could teach you if you wanted me to,' he said. He stepped close, waved his hands, spoke in a put-on spooky voice.

'Sleeeeep,' he said. 'Sleeeeeeep.'

He laughed. He flicked Mary's nose.

'Go on,' he said. 'Do it, man.'

'Leave her alone,' I said.

'Leave her alone,' he echoed in a little childish voice. He came closer. 'I could do it to you and all,' he said. 'I could put you under just like that. I could make you think anything I wanted you to think.'

We stared at each other. I clenched my fists, ready to battle again.

'Mebbe I've already done it,' he said, 'and you don't know. Mebbe you're sitting on a chair like Crazy is and you're in a dream and you're like putty in my hands. Sleeep. Sleeeeep.'

'Piss off, Stephen,' I said.

I grabbed his collar.

'Try it and I'll kill you,' I said.

He tried to smile. He shook his head.

'I wouldn't,' he said. 'I wouldn't, Davie. Believe me.'

'What happened to your mam and dad?' I said.

'What's that got to do with anything?'

'Dunno. Lots.'

He spat on the floor.

'I killed me dad then I drove me mother mad,' he said. 'Is that what you want to hear?'

'Dunno.'

'Dunno, dunno. Listen to you!'

I let him go. I started to turn away, but he caught my arm.

'I need you, Davie,' he said.

I tugged free.

'I do,' he said.

I turned back, and we looked into each other's eyes.

'When I'm with you,' he said, 'I know that I can be different. I know that I can be more than I am by myself.'

I sighed. It was true. And I knew that I could be different as well. I knew that when I was with him, I could be more than I was by myself. I knew that something had drawn us together, that somehow we were meant to be together. There was no going back to the life I'd had before. Not till I'd gone through what I had to go through with Stephen Rose.

'So we'll do it on Saturday,' he said.

'Aye. Saturday. Now wake Mary up.'

He woke her up. She smiled, touched by confusion and wonder.

'Don't do it again,' I said. 'She's not a toy.'

'I won't, Davie,' he said.

'Saturday,' I said.

'In the cave. After dark. I'll be there.'

'I'll be there. Goodbye, Miss Doonan.'

I headed back through the house to the door.

'But your jam and bread!' called poor Crazy Mary.

Three

Thirty

Saturday night. Lie on my bed, wait in the dark. No moon. The TV rumbles in the room below. I hear Dad's barks of laughter. Hell is on my mind, its searing flames, its savage devils, its prodding, poking, sniggering imps. I hear the howls and tears of the sinners. I imagine an eternity in Hell, time going on for ever and for ever without an end, with no chance of release or relief. 'Let me believe in nowt,' I whisper. 'Let there be life and nowt but life. Let the body be nowt but clay. Let God be gone. Let the soul be nowt but an illusion. Let death be nowt but rotting flesh and crumbling bones.' I touch the locket. 'Let this be nowt but stains and dust and Sellotape and shreds of cloth.' Dad's laughter rises from below again. 'Let nowt matter,' I say. 'Let it all be nowt but a bliddy joke. God, world, soul, flesh. Jokes, nowt but bliddy stupid jokes. Nowt but nowt, bliddy nowt.'

Soon they come upstairs. Mam puts her head round the door.

'Night night, son,' she whispers. 'Night night.'

I pretend to sleep. I don't say good night back until she's gone again and closed the door again and then I want to cry and call out,

'Mammy! Come back, Mammy!'

But I go on lying there. I try to empty my head of everything, try to enter a place where there's nothing: no world, no house, no room, no Davie. But it's Davie, of course, who rises from the bed an hour later, Davie who quietly puts on his clothes, who picks up the locket, who steps from his room, creeps downstairs, hesitates at the front door, Davie who opens the door and holds it open and lets the cold night air into the house, Davie who wants his mam to call, 'What you doing, Davie?', Davie who wants his dad to stamp downstairs and stop him and haul him back, Davie who closes the door behind him when none of this happens, Davie who steps out alone into the night.

Thirty-One

Folk have gone early to their beds. The streets of Felling are deserted. Lights burn in just a couple of upstairs windows. Streetlights are pale and orange. They hardly light the dark beneath the trees that line the lanes. The Swan is all in darkness. A few cars rumble on the unseen by-pass. The sound of singing comes from somewhere far away – maybe a family party stretching into the small hours, maybe a wedding or a wake. I try to move as if to cause the least disturbance: breathe shallowly, step gently, hardly swing my arms. I hear growling from a garden and I force myself to keep from flinching. It comes again, from closer by. I keep on walking, stepping gently. It growls again, whatever it is, from close behind. 'Don't run,' I breathe. It growls again and I turn my eyes and see it in the roadway, a pitch-black shape padding on all fours. It moves ahead and when I'm closer to the garden it turns to face me from the gate. Stands there, eyes glittering, teeth gleaming, saliva dangling from its open gob.

'Good boy,' I mutter. 'Good boy.'

It doesn't move. I open my empty hands, show them.

'Look,' I'm telling it. 'I'm safe. I'm no threat to you.'

It growls, steps closer.

'Please don't,' I whisper. 'Good boy. Good boy.'

It keeps coming. It keeps growling.

I crouch, and run my hand across the earth. I touch one of the broken jagged stones from Braddock's house. I grip it, yank it out of the soil. I raise it as the creature comes at me, and I bring it down across its skull. I strike again, again. It yelps, whimpers, slithers away from me. It turns its head, looks back at me, I raise the stone again, it slithers on.

I throw the stone away and hurry through the gate.

Thirty-Two

'Stop!' says Stephen.

He's in the cave, surrounded by lighted candles. His hand is raised.

'We got to do everything properly,' he says. 'We got to turn this to a holy place.'

I hesitate at the entrance.

'You should cross yourself,' he says. 'And ask for your sins to be washed away.'

I do this, then I reel and shudder. There's a body on the floor. Then I see it's not a body. It's a heap of clay, turning into the shape of a man: a bulk of torso, legs, arms, a clumsy head. I want to run. But Stephen laughs.

'That's him,' he says. 'Or half of him. Say hello. And careful you don't tread on him.'

I daren't look down as I step over him.

'You got out the house OK?' says Stephen.

'Aye. There was a dog or something outside.'

'There's always dogs round this place. You got the body and blood?'

'Aye.'

I pass him the locket. He clicks it open, inspects the things inside, sighs with pleasure.

'I couldn't get the whole things,' I say.

'That don't matter. The power's in the tiniest bits of it.' He puts the locket on a shelf in the rock. 'You done good. You'll be rewarded. Now put this on.'

He hands me a white shift. There's a moon and a sun and stars and a cross painted on it. He's got another for himself.

'You just put it on like this,' he says. 'I made them from one of Crazy's sheets.'

He pulls his over his head. It hangs down nearly to his knees.

'Go on, Davie,' he says. 'We got to do it all properly if we want it to work properly.'

I pull mine on.

'We look like bliddy priests,' I say.

'Aye, but like the ancient priests.'

'What do you mean, ancient?'

'This is how it started, Davie. All the churches and the mumbo jumbo and the useless Father O'Bliddy Mahoneys. There was no Bennett Colleges back then. There was no St Patrick's Churches. There was no soft soppy Masses and people in their best clothes saying stupid prayers. Back at the start it was priests finding their powers in the wilderness. It was folk like us, folk with power, folk in caves working magic, folk that was half-wild, folk truly close to God. Tonight you'll be an ancient priest, Davie. Tonight you'll work your magic on the world.' And he rolls his eyes towards the sky and spreads his arms and says, 'Allow the power of the universe to work through us tonight. On your knees, Davie!' He draws me down to kneel beside him. He takes my hand and rests it on the body of the half-completed clay man.

'This is our creature, Davie,' he says. 'Tonight we will make it, and make it live, and make it walk into the world.' And he leans down and speaks to the creature's head. 'This is Davie,' he says. 'He'll be your master just like me.' He grins at me. 'Now, Davie. More clay.'

So we dig more clay out of the clay pond. We kneel and turn the sticky sloppy clay into the shape of a man. And we become engrossed in it, and sometimes I forget myself and where I am, and I forget how crazy this would seem if someone else from Felling stumbled into the quarry tonight. We keep telling each other: 'Make him beautiful.' We keep packing more clay on to the body. 'Make him strong,' we say. We run our damp fingers across the surface of the man: 'Make it smooth like living skin.' We keep leaning back from our work. We smooth out the flaws, we touch in details, we smile and sigh at the beauty of our work. Before we finish the man's chest Stephen presses a wizened rose hip there to make a heart. We close the chest and rake the shapes of ribs with our fingertips. We put a conker inside the skull for a brain. We form the features of his face. Sycamore seeds make eyes, ash keys make the ears, dried-out hawthorn berries make nostrils, twigs and grass stems make his hair.

'We plant him like a garden,' Stephen says. 'We fill him with the sources of life. And this . . .' He lifts the locket. 'This'll make his soul.'

He hesitates. We look down at the man, gleaming gently in the candlelight.

'Where's the seat of the soul?' says Stephen.

'When I was little I used to think it was in the heart,' I say.

'But some'll tell you it's in the brain.'

'Mebbe it's everywhere.'

'Mebbe it doesn't matter. We put it somewhere, and life'll spread out from it.'

I press my fingers into the man's belly, and open up a space.

'Put it here, eh?' I say. 'Somewhere near where his centre is.'

And Stephen slips it deep inside, and closes the man's flesh again.

We kneel and look, in awe at what we've done. The man's so beautiful, so smooth, so strong. I feel the clay on the skin of my hands tightening as it dries.

'What now?' I say.

'We watch. And we pray.' He passes his hand before my eyes. 'And we believe, Davie. We believe in our power to make a man.' He passes his hand before my eyes again. 'You will see amazing things tonight.'

And the moon rises, creeping over the quarry's rim, casting its light into our cave and on to us and on to the dead-still body on the floor.

'Move, my creature,' murmurs Stephen.

And I murmur in time with him.

'Move, my creature. Move and live.'

Thirty-Three

And time passes and we pray and we implore and nothing happens. And the moon climbs until it hangs dead still and its reflection is shining bright at the dead centre of the clay pond. And bats move across it, and owls, and little pale moths. And our man lies there so still and the gleam fades on him as he dries, and often I touch him and know that he could be such a lovely creature if he lives and so I keep on praying that he'll live. And time passes and our whispers change and waver and become like weird singing that comes out of us but that's somehow not part of us, but is part of the night, the air, the moonshine, and the words in the singing are no longer like words but are just sounds drawn from somewhere deep inside ourselves, like creatures' cries, like complicated birdsong, nighttime birdsong. And we ourselves become somehow not ourselves, but we turn subtler, weirder, less attached to our bodies, less attached to our names. And often I look across the body lying on the floor to Stephen and expect to see him gone, or to see him turned to a shadow or a spirit without any substance to him. And he shimmers and sways, and he does seem to move in and out of sight, so we keep looking at each other, as if to keep each other here in the quarry, here in the world. And between us nothing happens, the man stays lying there on the floor dead still.

'At Bennett,' says Stephen, and his voice is a wavery squeaky distant thing, 'there was a little bunch of us, a little secret bunch. We used to meet together in the night, just like I'm meeting with you now. One night a kid called Joseph Wilson disappeared. One moment he was with us in a cupboard in the night, then he was just gone.'

I manage to make a word.

'Gone?'

'Half a night and half a day. We thought he was dead. We thought he'd been carried body and soul into the world of the spirits. The priests next morning thought that he must have fled from the place in the night when everybody was fast asleep. Then he was seen next day staggering through the birch trees in the college grounds. Clothes all torn, eyes all wild. Remembered nowt. Took him days to get his senses back, and even then he couldn't tell nobody what had happened, where he'd gone.'

'That's why you were thrown out?'

'No, that time they threw him out, and telt us he was a bad influence on us. Then another kid. Danny Keegan. He drew a thing out of the night.'

I just look at him.

'A little stumpy thing with horns. We were messing about in the night again and we were praying and conjuring and Danny found it running under his feet. We tried to catch it but it ran, then we seen it in the corridor, flapping wings, flying away. Danny said he'd been praying, "Send me a sign, Lord." '

'You did all sorts at Bennett?'

'Seems that long ago. We were little kids, took from home. Aye, we did all sorts till they trapped us.'

'How did they do that?'

'They sent a viper. Logan. Smooth and smarmy. He was one of the older ones, nearly ready to be a proper priest. He's working in a parish in Jarrow now. He tricked us. He said he could give us secrets, the secrets that were supposed to be kept from us till we were old. Secrets of life and death and when Christ would come again and what the saints knew and what the Pope keeps hidden from the rest of the world. So we let him come to us in the night and we did things with him like levitating tables and doing ouija boards and doing trances and hypnosis, and we telt him about Joseph and Danny and about a kid called Plummer that could hold his breath for half an hour and talk to ghosts. We should've knew. He was a spy. He telt the priests. They said it was me that led the others to the sinners' path. And so they sent me home.'

He leans down, runs his fingers across the lovely body.

'They telt me I was evil, Davie. They telt me I was an agent of the devil.'

His eyes are glittering in the candlelight.

'Do you think I'm evil?'

I shake my head. I pray. I touch the body. I look up at the moon. It hasn't moved.

'Live,' I whisper. 'Live and move.'

And our voices rise again, and begin a weird wordless song again, and the body between us stays dead still.

Thirty-Four

And we sprinkle ashes on the man, for Stephen says that he might rise like new life from the old, and we sprinkle water from the clay pond on him for we think he might grow like seed, and I lean right over him and breathe into his nostrils like the Lord God did when he formed man from the dust of the earth, and we whisper weirdly and we stand and sway and we start dancing and we beg him and implore and I begin to think that nowt will happen this night, that nowt will ever happen, and then Stephen starts talking about the night that he went home again.

'I was sent back home in a car. No time to think, to pray, to confess or say goodbye. Can you believe it? One day I was in, the next I was cast out. And I left the heavy doors and all the boys and all the priests and all the prayers and the smell of piss and all the jam and bread and the trees and we went out past the pond through the ancient gates and headed back to Whitley Bay. The priest that was with me was pointy-nosed, sloppy-lipped, miserable and old. He never once looked at me but whispered prayers all the way to Whitley Bay. And Mam and Dad didn't know what was coming to them. Mam was boiling bacon in the kitchen, Dad was planting cabbages in the garden. I left the car with the priest and with my ancient suitcase in my hand. He give them a letter with my sins in it. "Here is a devil, come back home again," he said. "Protect yourselves." And he was gone.'

And Stephen points down at the man and raises his voice: 'Move! Live!' And his voice echoes in the cave and out into the quarry and the night, but nowt happens to the man of clay.

'And your mam and dad,' I start. 'How did they . . .?'

'Cried their hearts out. Floods of tears. They said they had tried to live right. They had tried to bring me up right. And I said that mebbe all that trying to do right was what was wrong. Mebbe we should have lived crazy like all the Roses, mebbe we should go now and live in a tent in Plessey Woods like Rocky did and get hairy and wild and scary and scared. And Dad shook me and said, "You cannot mean that!" And I said I did and they wept more floods and Mam held me and telt me to confess to her the things I'd done.'

'And did you?'

'I telt her some things, aye. I telt her that loads of the things that were writ in the letter were lies. I telt her a few of me own truths and a few of me own lies. In the end I started to forget myself which parts of it were truth and which parts were lies. Pretty soon, looking back at the days and nights at Bennett was like looking back into a time of dreams and it was like there was no way of knowing where the truth was, and certainly no way of knowing what was right and what was wrong. But we settled. We stayed on in the little terraced house in Whitley Bay and didn't head out to the woods. I went to school and I was like just any of them kids that's come back from a place like Bennett – a little bit distracted, a little bit wild. They went on with their jobs. She was a waitress in a Tilly's Tea Shack next to the sea. He cleaned the machines in a factory that made tyres in Blyth. Everything went on like everything was normal and we were normal people living normal lives. But there was too much bubbling inside. Mam started swigging bottles of sherry and smashing cups and plates on the kitchen floor. She shaved all her hair off and started talking about slashing her wrists. I was scribbling spells on me bedroom walls and calling spirits out the night. I got expelled from school for calling a curse down on the headmaster and saying God had died in

1945. Dad just couldn't stand it all. He said we should all go to Australia and start again, then one night we were eating a steak and kidney pudding and watching *Look North* and he had a stroke and died.'

He pauses and gazes through the flickering light at me, like he's checking if I'm following him, if I'm keeping up with him.

'You were there?' I ask.

'Sitting across the table from him, Davie. Close to him as I am to you now. I thought he was choking on his pudding, but he wasn't. He fell off his chair and died.'

We're silent for a time. We sit on the cave floor beside the man.

'I'm sorry,' I whisper.

'It's OK,' says Stephen.

But I look across, and see that Stephen Rose has started to cry.

Thirty-Five

'Did you ever see anybody die?' whispers Stephen.

I shake my head.

'Me neither till that night. It was like there was a sudden storm inside him, then the look of terror in his eyes, then the gasping of his breath, then the drop, then nothing more. By the time me and Mam was kneeling at him, everything had stopped. No breath, no pulse, no heart, no nowt at all. He was dead and still as this lovely man is now. And already turning cold, already turning back to clay.'

He lets his tears fall again and we're silent.

'I could have saved him, Davie,' he says. 'If only Mam hadn't gone mental on me.'

'What?' I say.

'She was howling. She was all for running straight out into the night, straight out to the phone box across the street. "We got to get an ambulance," she said.

"Wait," I telt her. "I can bring him back again." I grabbed her arm. But she was far gone. She walloped me with her open hand. She ran out into the street. I seen her through the window, in the phone box, jabbering stupidly down the phone. I locked the front door on her. I lay down with Dad. I talked into his ear. I called on his spirit. "Come back to us. Come back into the world, Dad." I held his head between my hands. I called on the powers of the moon and the stars and the sun and the whole universe. I called on the power of God himself. "Send my father back to us!" '

He looks down at his hands, as if he can still see his dad's head between them. He looks across at me and his eyes are weird and wild.

'This is true, Davie. This is as true as we're together in this cave in this quarry in this night. Tell me you believe me.'

'What happened?'

'Tell me you believe me and you'll know.'

I stare back at him. He waits for me. And I say the true and crazy words.

'Yes. I believe you.'

'Yes!' he gasps. 'I hold me dad and I call him back, and it starts happening, Davie. I feel the life coming back into him. I feel his spirit move. I feel a tiny breath. I feel a faint faint beating of his heart. And oh, Davie,

he's coming back to me and it's so so wonderful . . .
Then the door's broke down and the ambulance men is
shoving me away and thumping me dad's chest and he's
dead again.'

He sighs.

'And me mam's hands is clamped across her face and
she's jabbering and mental and she's looking at me like
the mental one is me.'

And we look at each other, and there's dead silence
in the cave, and there's no more shifting, no more
shimmering. Stephen Rose, and I, are definitely there,
in the cave, in the quarry, in Braddock's ancient Garden.
And I watch Stephen Rose lean forward and whisper
into the ear of the clay man lying on the floor.

'Now. Come into the world. Come to me, to Stephen
Rose. I call on you. Live, my creature. Move.'

And I see the man move. His limbs twitch, he turns
his head, and looks straight into Stephen Rose's eyes.

Thirty-Six

What would you do? Kneel there while a slab of the dead earth starts coming to life before your eyes? Kneel there and just watch while a man of clay shifts his shoulders and rolls his neck like he's stretching himself awake after a long sleep? Kneel there and say, 'Haven't we done a brilliant thing, Stephen Rose? Haven't we got amazing powers?' Stephen's transfigured. He's filled with dreadful joy. One hand points to Heaven, the other points down to our creature. He whimpers and howls and prays and sings. Me? I'm off. I jump across the two of them. I slither through the clay pond, struggle through the quarry, through the hawthorn, through the fallen gates and stand on Watermill Lane beneath the moon, surrounded by silvery rooftops, pitch-black windows, dead-still gardens, and over everything is Felling's deep dark silence. I expect to be struck down there, to die. I expect the earth to open up and grisly clawing hands to reach up and drag me down to Hell. But there's nowt. I rip the shift off and use it to wipe the muck off myself. I throw it through the gates, back into the garden, then I run on all alone, my footsteps falling on the solid earth, echoing from the sleeping houses. I creep back into my house, back into my bed. I tell myself to tell myself it's all a vision or a dream. I tell myself to tell myself that none of it's happened really but that I've been in bed all this time, that I saw an imaginary boy called Davie doing imaginary things with an imaginary creature out in an imaginary night. I tell myself not to scream, to stop whimpering, to stop trembling. I tell myself that come the morning everything will be all right. And then it's morning and Mam's yelling upstairs at me and telling me it's time for church, time for me to get ready for the altar. And I wash and dress myself and go downstairs and stand stupid and pale as they ask if I'm all right.

'Aye!' I snap. 'I am all right.'

And they roll their eyes and shake their heads and turn from me and start talking about some dog.

'Dog?' I say.

'Aye,' says Dad. 'Miss O'Malley's poor dog.'

'Boris,' says Mam. 'Her lovely Labrador.'

'Seems some bugger bludgeoned it in the night,' says Dad.

'Poor Boris,' says Mam. 'Poor Miss O'Malley.'

'Who'd believe it?' says Dad.

'Here in Felling,' says Mam. 'Who'd believe it?'

I leave the house, head for church. A brilliant morning. No wind. Bright terrifying penetrating light. People hurrying through the streets, filled with friendliness and goodness. 'Morning, Davie,' they call as they pass by. 'Hello, son,' as they touch me kindly on the shoulder.

Geordie and I don't look at each other, don't speak, as we put our cassocks and cottas on.

'You two all right?' says Father O'Mahoney.

'Aye, Father,' says Geordie.

'That's grand,' says the priest, and he turns from us and lowers his head and murmurs his prayers.

All through Mass, I think I'm keeling over, falling, passing out. When Communion comes, I lower my head and won't take it. Father O'Mahoney whispers, 'Davie?' but I squeeze my eyes shut and keep my head down and won't take it. I hold the silver dish beneath the faces of friends and family and neighbours that I know so well, and my hand trembles as I gaze at all those faces lifted so innocently up to us.

After Mass I try to rush away, but Father O'Mahoney stands in front of me.

'Now, then, Davie,' he says, and his voice is tender, gentle.

'Yes, Father,' I whisper.

'Are you all right, Davie?'

'Aye, Father.'

'Are you happy?'

'Don't know, Father.'

He rests his hand on my head.

'It's a grand life,' he says.

'Aye, Father.'

'But it was never designed to be easy.'

'No, Father.'

'That's grand, then.' He sighs and stares at the ceiling and ponders. 'I think you were not at confession last night, Davie?'

'No, Father.'

'Maybe you should come soon.'

'Yes, Father.'

'Yes, Father. That's grand, then. Now, go on, catch up with your pal.'

I go out of the vestry, through the church, out of the front door. Dozens of people stand about in the courtyard, talking and laughing. I try to move through without being seen. I hear Frances and Maria laughing. I hear Mam calling out to me. I try to ignore her. Then there's an intake of breath nearby, a burst of low concerned chattering.

'Dead?' someone whispers. 'Dead?'

Then Mam's at my side.

'What's wrong?' I say.

'A dreadful thing. A boy has been found dead.'

I close my eyes, don't breathe, don't speak.

'His name,' she says, 'is Martin Mould.'

Thirty-Seven

Next thing I know I'm on Watermill Lane, part of a scattered crowd that stands beneath the trees, leans against hedges, sits on benches and on low front garden walls. We stand singly and in little gossiping groups. I'm alone, ignored, terrified. There's two police cars parked in the roadway. There's a policeman guarding the entrance to Braddock's Garden. The silver on his helmet glitters in the Sunday morning sun. He stands with his legs astride, with his arms crossed. He keeps turning his head to look back into the garden. The other policemen are inside.

I want to yell, 'Get them out! The monster'll get them and you as well! Run! Run!'

Somebody pokes me in the ribs. I turn. Geordie. He has the marks on his face from our fight.

'Dead!' he whispers.

He keeps his face straight. He makes a fist and widens

his eyes. 'Dead, Davie!' He allows a grin to cross his face. He lowers his voice further. 'A bliddy dream come true!'

Then Mam and Dad come to us and Geordie's face is straight again.

'Seems some lads found him,' says Dad. 'Seems he must have gone over the quarry edge.' He lowers his voice. 'There was an ambulance earlier. Took his body away.'

'He went over?' I say. 'Fell, you mean?'

'Must have. Probably some time in the night. Story is he'd have been full of . . .'

'Poor soul,' says Mam.

'Aye. You two have much to do with him?' says Dad.

'Not if we could help it,' says Geordie.

'Troublemaker?' says Dad.

'Hard as nails,' says Geordie.

'I've heard,' says Dad. 'And all that drinking for a lad of his . . .'

'He fell?' I say.

'Aye. Poor lad. He fell.'

'He was dead scary,' I say.

'Aye?' says Dad.

'Aye!' I say. 'Definitely!'

'Hush,' says Mam. She puts her arm around me. 'Don't speak ill of the dead, Davie.'

'It'll be the end of the garden, anyway,' says Dad. 'There's nowt now that'll stop them shutting it up and filling it in.'

We all look towards the gates.

'It's always been a place of danger,' Mam says.

'And adventure,' says Dad.

'Aye,' she says. 'And adventure. All the way back to when we were . . . Oh, look!'

Another police car draws up. A little shuffling woman steps out of it. A policewoman helps her towards the gates. The whisper travels through the crowd.

'It's Mrs Mould,' says Mam. 'Oh, poor soul.'

The policewoman leads the woman into the garden.

'She just wants to see the place,' says Mam. There's tears in her eyes. 'Wouldn't you just?' She holds me tight, as if protecting me. I hold my breath. I wait for the screams. I wait for them to come running out in terror with the monster coming after them, but nowt happens, and all around the pity and the gossiping intensify.

'Poor soul,' says Mam again. She turns to her friends, talks and whispers with them again. 'Oh!' she says. 'I know. It's such a sad sad tale.'

I turn my eyes to her. A sad sad tale? With a brute like Mouldy in it?

She clicks her tongue, nods, shrugs.

'It's common knowledge down in Pelaw. The dad worked as a welder in the yards. He fell into a ship's tank, broke his back and quickly died. The battle for compensation lasted years, as these things always do. But it come at last, a few hundred pounds, a pittance set against what had been lost. By then, though, Mrs Mould was frail and drained, the boy was growing wild, she had no control of him. Who's to know what pain and loss'll do to any family and to any heart. The boy turned young to drink. Seems she couldn't refuse him the cash for it. He was big and strong and he looked like a man and there was plenty pity for them, so many looked the other way. And now he's fallen, too, and she's lost him, too. And what's she left with now, sad soul?'

We watch the gates. Nowt happens.

'And she won't want us lot standing gawping,' she says. 'Come on. Let's go back home.'

I stand a moment more, watching, waiting. Nowt happens. The sunlight pours down upon the world, so bright and so clear. I reach down and scratch a little dirt from the verge. I hold it in my palm. 'Move,' I mutter, and of course nowt happens. Everything outside this morning on Watermill Lane seems imaginary, unreal, a thing of dream. I try to tell myself that the tragedy across the road has nowt to do with me. Mouldy was drunk. He fell. And me? I try to tell myself that I've been fooled, I've been deceived, I've been hypnotised, I've been . . .

'Davie?' says Mam.

'Aye.'

I let the soil fall back to earth. I stand up and start walking away with her and Dad.

Crazy Mary's at her garden gate with Stephen at her side. Her eyes widen as we approach.

'It's the good altar boy!' she says. 'And his lovely mam and dad.'

'Hello, Mary,' says Mam. She rests a hand on Mary's forearm. Mary beams, delighted. 'Are you all right now, Mary?'

'Aye,' says Mary. 'I just woke up!'

She holds Mam's hand.

'What's happening across there?' she whispers.

'Oh, a little bit of trouble, Mary.'

Stephen looks at me, so calm.

'While all of us were in our beds,' he says.

'Aye!' says Mary. 'Would you believe it? I just woke up!'

A look of wonder passes across her face.

'And such a funny dream!' she says.

She closes her eyes, and puts a hand to her head as if to pluck the memory from the darkness in her.

'A monster!' she says.

'A monster?' says Mam.

'Aye! A monster come into my house! Heeheehee! It did!'

She opens her eyes and holds her hand across her mouth and giggles and grins.

'Great clarty footprints all through the hall! Heeheehee! And now he's sleeping in the shed. He is! Heeheehee! He is!'

Thirty-Eight

That afternoon, two policemen come. Dad goes to the door but it's me they want to see. He brings them in. One of them's called Sergeant Fox, the other's PC Ground. They stand there with their helmets under their arms and their notebooks and pencils in their hands. They won't sit down.

'Now then, son,' says Sergeant Fox. 'A couple of questions, then we'll be on our way.'

'Nothing to worry about,' says PC Ground.

'OK,' I say.

'Number one,' says Sergeant Fox. 'Did you know the lad who died?'

'A bit,' I whisper.

'Speak up, Davie,' says Mam.

'Yes,' I say.

I'm trembling. Inside, I'm screaming.

'Very good,' says Sergeant Fox. 'Now then. *What*

did you know of him?

'Like what?' I say.

'Like, what kind of lad he was. What he got up to. His . . . interests, things like that.'

'His inner life, so to speak,' says PC Ground.

I shrug.

'Dunno,' I say.

'He kept well away from him,' says Dad.

'Is that right?' says Sergeant Fox.

'Aye,' I say. 'I was . . .'

'You were . . .?' says Sergeant Fox.

'Scared,' I say.

The policemen scribble in their books.

'And when did you see him last?' says Sergeant Fox.

I search my memory.

'Friday. After school. Outside The Swan. He was . . .'

'Drunk?' says PC Ground.

I nod. They sigh and shake their heads. They know. He often was. They whisper with Mam and Dad, then turn to me again.

'Was he a bother to you?' asks PC Ground.

'Sometimes,' I say.

'That's why he kept away from him,' says Dad.

'Correct,' says Sergeant Fox. 'We've spoken to your pal George Craggs. He put us in the picture.'

'Now, then,' says Sergeant Fox. He flicks through his

204

notes. It's now that I expect them to bring out the painted shift, to start asking me about what happened in the cave last night, to start talking about a clay monster, to start asking me what I know about a dog. But nowt happens.

'It's a sad sad do,' says the sergeant.

He looks into my eyes.

'Anything else you want to tell us?' he says.

'Any important-looking facts and figures?' says PC Ground.

'No,' I say.

Sergeant Fox touches my shoulder.

'Don't take it to heart,' he says. 'Such things happen. We grow away from them. They're mebbe even part of . . .'

'Growing up,' says PC Ground.

Dad takes them to the door. I hear him say that I'm a sensitive sort, but I'll get over it.

Mam hugs me.

'We'll send some flowers to Martin's mam,' she says.

She shivers.

'There but for the grace of God,' she says.

Thirty-Nine

That night I wake up and something draws me to the window. I pull back the curtains and see the monster. There he is, down in the street. He's under a streetlight, staring back at me. He's massive, a huge dark shadow. I know he wants me to go to him. I know he wants me to speak to him. I hear a voice inside me:

You are the one who made me, Master. I am yours.

'Go away!' I whisper. 'I don't want you!'

He doesn't move.

What do you want of me, Master?

'Nothing! Get lost! Turn back to clay!'

He lowers his head and walks heavily away from the streetlight and into the dark.

'Stay away!' I whisper. 'Jump back into the clay pond. Go away and bliddy die!'

Forty

Geordie's waiting for me at the school gate next morning. He goes on like there's never been anything wrong between us, like the battle between us never happened. He grabs me and puts his arm round me.

'A dream come bliddy true!' he says.

I pull away from him. He grins.

'I know,' he says. 'I know. It's awful and he had an awful life and all that stuff but it don't change the fact he was a bliddy monster.'

'Was he?' I say.

'Be honest, man. Did a little bit of you not start cheering when you heard?'

'No.'

'No? Are you sure? Right from the start we said it – the world'd be a better place if he was gone. Even Skinner and Poke's pleased about it – not that they'll admit it yet.'

'How do you know that?'

'I seen them yesterday. I could tell. They could hardly keep their faces straight. It was them that found him. They'd planned to meet up in the quarry early yesterday morning and wait for us and ambush us. Mouldy must have got there first when it was hardly light and he goes straight over the bliddy edge.'

We walk across the yard. Geordie breathes deeply and turns his face towards the brilliant sky.

'It's a new world!' he says, then he stops dead still. 'You know what this could do, Davie. Don't you?'

'What?'

'It could put an end to all the battling. Skinner and Poke might turn into our mates. The truce could turn into a proper peace. The Pelaw/Felling war could be over. It could all be in the past. And all cos one kid's gone and died. Pretty good, eh?'

I walk on. He catches up with me and laughs.

'Mind you,' he says. 'Dunno if I really want all that!' Then he clenches his fists as we go inside. 'It is! A dream come bliddy true!'

Forty-One

Last lesson of the day, and Prat's all blather again. Clay and creativity and striding about the classroom and closing his eyes and staring at the sky and clay pellets and jelly babies flying around his head.

'You can go too far,' I say when he's in mid-stream.

He blinks and looks at me.

'Sorry, Davie?' he says.

'You can go too far. You can create too much.'

He comes to my table, leans over me, delighted.

'For example, Davie?'

'Well . . .' I look down. I stumble over the thoughts, the words. 'Some of the things that we create are . . .'

'Are?' he prompts me.

'Some of the things that we create are . . . destructive.'

'Exactly!' He punches the air and spins away. 'The things that we create – some of them, many of them – are themselves destructive!'

He looks around the room, scans the faces.

'Such as?' he says.

'Guns,' he is told.

'Bullets,' he is told.

'Poisons.'

'Nerve gas.'

'Bombs.'

'The nuclear bomb.'

'War itself.'

'Exactly!' says Prat. 'Exactly! Exactly! Exactly!'

He closes his eyes. He taps his forehead. We know that he's about to tell us something that he thinks is dead profound.

'It is the human paradox,' he says. 'We are creative beings. But our passion to create goes hand in hand with our passion to destroy.' He claps his hands together, makes a double fist. 'And the passions are linked as tight as this.'

Then he shuts up for a while.

'Thank God,' says Geordie. 'What the Hell did you get him started for?'

I roll a lump of clay hopelessly around my table. I find Maria watching me and she seems so cold, so distant. I look away from her, through the window, across the yard. It's a misty afternoon. I see the monster at the distant iron boundary fence. He grips the bars and looks towards me. I hear his voice inside my head.

I am yours, Master. Tell me what to do.

'No,' I gasp.

'What's up with you?' says Geordie.

'What things will we create,' says Prat, 'when our ability to create intensifies? What monsters will we make?'

I watch my monster striding alongside the fence, seeking a way in.

'I,' says Prat, 'am an optimist. I believe that the forces of good will defeat the forces of evil.'

The monster lurches towards the gate.

'What's *up*?' says Geordie.

'But could it be,' says Prat, 'that the end of creativity will be to make a thing that will turn back upon us and destroy us?'

He goggles at me.

'What do *you* think, Davie? Could that be human destiny – that we are driven to create our own destruction?'

Far beyond him, the monster's almost in.

'Dunno, sir,' I say. 'I've got to go, sir. I've got to bliddy go.'

And I push my chair away, and shove Prat aside, and I run.

Forty-Two

I run alongside the by-pass. I run into the graveyard. I shelter by the Braddock graves. I pray. I want to turn back time, to go back to the past, to go back to the days that suddenly seem so long ago, the days of being an ordinary kid, the days before the arrival of Stephen Rose, the days before the monster. I watch the graveyard gate, the shadows. I watch for the monster. I snarl at myself, at how pathetic I am. I leave the graveyard and head for Crazy Mary's house. I knock at the door but there's no answer. I peep through the window and see Crazy sitting at the table and goggling into space. I knock again. Stephen comes. He lets me in.

'We been waiting,' he says. 'What took so long?'

He leads me past motionless Mary and into the garden and into the shed. Sunlight slants down through the glass in the roof and the edges and corners are deep in shadow.

I'm trembling again.

'What we going to do?' I say.

'You're in a state, Davie,' he says. 'You got to calm down.'

'I seen him,' I say.

'Him?'

'The monster. He come last night.'

'Mebbe you were imagining it, Davie.'

'And he came this afternoon, at school.'

'That can't be true.'

'It is, Stephen. It's true. It really worked. We really did make a monster.'

'I know that, Davie. Cos look – he's been in here with me all the time.'

And he holds his hand towards a corner and now I see the monster standing there: dead still, eyes closed, massively-muscled, head touching the ceiling.

Stephen smiles.

'Say hello to your creation, Davie.'

I move out of the brilliant light, move into the shadow, stand beside the monster.

'You made another one,' I said.

I dare to touch him – bitter cold, clay cold.

'No, Davie. This is him. He come back with me out the quarry. He'll be safer here.'

I touch the monster's great hands. I imagine them clenched tight around Mouldy's neck.

'What happened to Mouldy?' I say.

'He died, Davie. He fell.'

'Fell?'

'What else?' The smile plays across his face. 'He always was a clumsy lout.'

He comes into the shadow beside me.

'Our creature exists at the very edge of life,' he says. 'He is dormant now. It is only our belief and our will that will keep him from crumbling back into the earth. He needs our command, Davie. What shall we tell him to do?'

'Nothing,' I whisper.

'Mebbe we should at least give him a name.'

'Clay,' I whisper.

'That'll do. Hello, Clay.'

'Hello, Clay,' I whisper.

'That's right, Davie. Now, Davie, command him.'

You are my Master, I hear. *What will I do?*

'Nothing,' I whisper.

'Nothing means that he'll crumble back into the earth. Nothing'll be the end of him.'

The silence and stillness are deep as eternity. There's nothing beyond the three of us, beyond this shed.

'What are you?' I whisper.

'Me?' says Stephen.

'Yes, you.'

'A boy like you.'

'That's all?' I say.

'Are you saying that *I* am the monster?'

I stare at him. He smiles.

'And what are *you*?' he says.

'A boy,' I whisper. 'An ordinary boy.'

'A boy who can do wondrous things. Don't disappoint me, Davie. Calm down.' He passes his hand before my eyes. 'Command your creation, Davie.'

Master. What shall I do?

I stare at this astonishing thing. I can't resist.

'Move,' I whisper. 'Live, Clay. Move.'

And I feel the creature drawn back over the edge of life. And I feel the spirit moving in it.

'Live,' I whisper. 'Live.'

And it sways gently and turns its face to me.

Command me, Master.

And this time I don't run, but I meet its eye, and I force the words out of myself.

'Walk.'

And the monster walks across the shed through the glare beneath the glass and into the far shadow.

'Turn.'

And the monster turns.

'Walk.'

And it walks back through the light again and into

the shadow at my side. And Stephen Rose is laughing, like it's all a joke.

Then he takes a stiff clay angel, and holds it out.

'Take this, Clay,' he says.

And the creature takes it.

'Destroy,' says Stephen.

And the creature crushes the angel between its massive hands and the dust and fragments crumble to the floor and Stephen giggles and giggles again.

Forty-Three

'Be still, Clay,' I say, and the monster is still again. It stands beside us in the shadow. I touch it, lean close to it. Nothing moves in it.

'It can't be true,' I whisper.

'It is, Davie. Look at our creation. Clay lives. Clay moves. How can you deny it?'

'But it can't be true.'

'Mebbe God said that to himself,' said Stephen, 'on the morning he created us. It can't be true! I can't do this! But his creature stood up on the earth and God was flabbergasted by his own power. And the creature walked. And the creature dared to look God in the face. And God saw mischief in his creature's eye. And God was bothered by what he'd done. He said to hisself, "Mebbe this is a bliddy monster that I've made. What horrors have I unleashed upon my lovely world?" But it was too late. The deed was done.'

I touch our cold creation. It waits again for our instruction.

'He could have uncreated us,' I whisper. 'He could have destroyed us.'

'Aye, he could have. He even said he wanted to. Remember the tales? The folk he'd made were evil, they'd went all wrong, they were wreaking havoc in the world. They were driving God bliddy mental. He got filled with anger and vengeance. He sent down floods and fires and plagues. But that God, he was too good for his own good.'

I shudder. I watch the dust tumbling down endlessly through the light.

'He loved us, see?' says Stephen. 'He thought we were bliddy wonderful. He sent down the forces of destruction, but he couldn't bring hisself to destroy the lot of us. He always saved a few.'

'Like Noah and his family.'

'Aye, like them. And a few like them were supposed to make everything turn out right. Fat chance, eh? Pretty soon he's getting drove mental again by what's going on and he's sending down the fire and the brimstone and the bliddy plagues but nowt never turns out right and for centuries and centuries he's just getting mentaller and mentaller till one day he just says, "Right, I've had enough. I'm off." '

'Off?'

'Aye. He nicked off, Davie. He abandoned us. About 1945, I reckon.'

'1945?'

'Mebbe a bit earlier. You know: war, concentration camps, gas ovens, atom bomb, all that stuff. Enough to drive anybody away.'

I touch the creature's cheek. I hear its voice inside me.

I am yours, Master. Tell me what to do.

Stephen laughs. He points into the sky. Beyond the glass it is clear and unblemished blue.

'Remember when they used to tell us God was in the sky, Davie? You ever seen him up there?' He touches his chest. 'Remember when they used to say you'd find him in your heart? You ever found him there? Ever? Truly? He ever answer any of your prayers?'

I shrug. I lean on the creature.

'And in the church? You ever see him wandering there beside you on the altar?'

'But . . .' I say.

'He's gone. There's just emptiness, Davie. Emptiness, silence, nowtness, going on for ever. Mebbe he was here in the past, but these days, man, it's all a bliddy joke.'

'But the power of the Lord. The body and the blood. You said we needed them.'

'Aye, we did.' He comes in close. He breathes on me. The three of us – Stephen, me, Clay – are tight together in the shadows. 'But it was really you that needed them, Davie. I stuck the stupid trashy nick-nacks in him cos they helped you to believe. The power that made this thing was yours and mine, Davie, and nowt to do with God. We're on our own, Davie. And it's enough. We're the ones with power now.'

He grins, face almost pressing against mine.

I hear Clay.

Master, tell me what to do.

'But the angel,' I say.

'What angel?'

'The angel on the beach at Whitley Bay. The angel that . . .'

'Ahahahahahaha! Did you believe *that*? Ahahahahaha!'

I stare at him. He rubs the tears of laughter from his eyes.

'You're worse than I thought, Davie,' he says. 'I bliddy made that up.'

'But she . . .'

'You're a bliddy wonder, Davie. What an innocent.'

Master! What shall I do?

'Get him, Clay,' I whisper. The monster opens its eyes. I feel the life in it. 'Do something,' I say. It turns to Stephen. It raises its hands. 'Hurt the bastard!' I say.

And Clay does step forward, and Stephen does back away, but he's still smiling. He raises his own hand and says, 'Stop,' and Clay is motionless.

'See?' says Stephen. 'You wouldn't harm your maker, would you, Clay?'

He grins at me.

'You wouldn't even harm Martin Mould, would you, Clay?'

'Martin Mould?' I whisper.

'Martin Mould, Davie. Will I tell you what really happened to your dear departed Martin Mould?'

I lick my lips. I stare into Stephen's eyes.

'He fell,' I whisper. 'The police said that. Skinner and Poke said that.'

'Aye. Hahahaha! And I said that, didn't I, Davie? Well open your lugs, cos I'm going to tell you the real truth – and the funny thing is, nobody but you will ever think that the truth could possibly be true.'

Forty-Four

'You ran away, Davie. It's understandable, man. You didn't expect nowt to happen, did you? Not really. Or mebbe you did expect something to happen, but once it started it was all a bit too much for you. So you cleared off. Me, I was ready for it. I've been getting ready for this for years. I remember when I was little I telt me mam, I'm going to be a God when I grow up. She used to laugh. A devil, more like, she used to say. And she used to kiss me cheek. Funny little boy, she used to say. Funny little Stevie. Ha! Probly it was way back then she started heading round the twist. What d'you think, Davie?'

'Dunno.'

'Dunno? But then, how could you know? You and me's from different worlds, Davie. There's no way a good lad like you wanted to be like God. And no way a lovely mam like yours had the makings of madness in her. D'you ever think your mam was mental, Davie?'

I shake my head.

'Exactly, Davie.' Then he watches me in silence for a while. 'D'you ever think *you* was mental, Davie?'

I shake my head, then I stop. I look at Stephen, at Clay, at the empty sky, and the events of the last days move in me and in the shadows like ghosts and dreams. I want to run away again, to run back home, to scream and scream. Stephen answers his own question for me.

'Not till now, eh, Davie? Not till God was gone and Stephen Rose and Clay was on the scene. Never mind. The worry'll pass. Haha!'

He pokes me gently in the chest.

'Or mebbe it won't,' he says. 'Mebbe it'll be there for ever and ever and ever and . . . And mebbe on your deathbed you'll be asking yourself, "Did I go crackers when Stephen Rose arrived? Has everything since then just been a daft illusion?" '

I find that I'm leaning close to Clay, that my shoulder rests against his chest.

'Anyway, you ran away,' says Stephen. 'I don't blame you. You just did what God did, only a bit quicker. You didn't wait for time to pass and for your creature to start making mayhem. One look was enough for you, eh? I'm off! I'm back to me bed!'

He smiles.

'Stand back,' he says to Clay and Clay straightens up and backs into the shadows. Stephen pats his arm. 'That's right,' he says. 'Good lad. Stand still now.'

I follow Clay further into the shadows. He is cold, but he moves his arm to accommodate me, as if he's half-holding me.

Lean on me, Master. Tell me what to do.

'By the way,' says Stephen, 'I cleared up after you. Picked your priest's shift out of them thorn trees. Brought it back here. Just as well, eh? Could have been a bit of evidence for them.'

'Evidence for what?'

'Well, if they ever get to trying to implicate you in what happened.'

He laughs.

'Don't worry, man,' he says. 'You were in your bed that night, same as I was. The dog? That must've been Mouldy or some other nutter out in the middle of the night. Clay monster? Barmy. And Mouldy? Well, he fell, didn't he? He must have. Except he didn't fall, Davie.'

He smiles. I say nothing. Clay puts his other arm across my chest.

Lean on me, Master.

Stephen watches us.

'Ahhh,' he says. 'That's nice. Anyway, I heard you splashing and crashing away, Davie. I couldn't take much notice. I had to go on bringing this fine feller to life. And it mebbe didn't matter that you'd gone. You'd done your bit. I couldn't have done it without you.'

He pauses, smiles, ponders.

'It's true, Davie,' he says. 'I couldn't have done this on me own. I remember seeing you for the first time in the graveyard. There you were in your cassock and cotta. Now here's a likely-looking lad, I thought.'

He giggles. He grabs a lump of clay. He stabs eyes, nostrils, mouth into it with his finger. He wobbles the clay in the air.

'Hello,' he squeaks. 'Hello, Davie.' And he laughs. 'Remember, Davie?' he says. 'Remember how you said hello back to it. Oh, what a moment that was. This lad's been sent to me, I thought. Dead ordinary, dead innocent, dead big imagination. This is just the lad I need.'

He squashes the clay and puts it down again. I watch him. My fists clench. I want to fight him, to kill him, but I can't move as I follow his tale to its end.

'So,' he says. 'You're away, running through the clarts and the trees and back to your mam and dad and your bed. And here's our creature lifting hisself off the cave floor like he's saying, "Here I am, Master. What do you want me to do?" And he stands up and he's bliddy beautiful, so I think, well, let's just go for a walk and get to know each other and see what's what. So we set off wandering like a couple of merry bairns. And it's such a lovely night. Did you notice that, Davie? That great big shining moon and that lovely clear sky? But mebbe you were too distracted. So we leave the cave and the quarry and we're in the garden and I'm saying, Stop, Walk, Turn and teaching him all the stuff like that and I can't believe it's all happening, but it is. And time's passing and morning's not too far away and I'm starting to think of tomorrow and how I'm going to hide the bugger. Then there's footsteps in the garden. "Stop," I say. "In here," I say. And we get in under a tree and I'm looking out, and there he is. Mouldy. I can't believe it. But it's true. That's his great big ugly silhouette. That's him, stamping through the long grass and the weeds, coming straight towards me. And no, I can't believe me bliddy luck.' He pauses and ponders. 'Funny how Mouldy always seemed to be around just when I needed him. Like, remember how he drove you to me door that day?'

'Aye,' I answer.

'Aye. Ha, it's nearly like there was a purpose to him. Funny, eh . . .? Anyway, there he is. He cannot see us, of course. He would've passed straight by. But like I say, it's destiny. So I step out from under the tree and I says, "Hiya, Mouldy." He nearly drops dead but then he's back to being hard as nails again. "Who's there?" he grunts. "Me," I says. "Stephen Rose." And I see his eyes glittering in the moonlight. "Stephen bliddy Rose," he growls, and he starts coming at me and saying what he's going to do to me. "Oh," I say, "and there's me monster as well," and I turn around. "Howay out here," I say, and here comes this feller out from under the tree, and Mouldy nearly drops dead for a second time ... I'll give him this, your Martin Mould – he doesn't turn and run like ninety-nine-point-nine per cent would. He stands his ground, puts his fists up. Mebbe Martin Mould really was hard as nails. But mebbe thick as clarts is a better definition ... "This is our enemy," I say to Clay, then I say, "You got to destroy our enemy," and Mr Clay is after Mr Mould. Of course, Mouldy's not panicking and running and screaming. That'd be far too chicken for a big hard lad like him. He's backing off, backing off. And our lad's not much of a runner if the truth be told. But he's looking pretty determined, and he's going forward. "Kill," I say. "Kill the enemy. Kill! Kill!" And I'm laughing at Mouldy's face that's white as death beneath the moon. And pretty soon he's backed as far as he can go. He's at the quarry's edge and by now even hard-as-nails Mouldy is bliddy petrified and he cannot move an inch. "What is it?" he whispers. "It's me monster," I say. "Isn't he lovely?" I say. "Why don't you say hello?" I say. I wait a bit, but Mouldy says nowt. Just sort of jabbers and whimpers. "OK," I say. "Now me monster's going to kill you." And I say to Clay, "Kill him! Shove him over!" '

Stephen pauses. He reaches up and strokes Clay's cheek.

'Poor lad,' says Stephen. 'It was so confusing for you, wasn't it, Clay? Me going, "Kill! Kill! Kill!" and Mouldy like a little boy going, "Don't! Please don't!" Ha. That's mebbe what comes of having two makers. If you'd just been mine, I doubt you would've hesitated. But there's too much of the Davie in you . . .'

I lean on Clay.

'He didn't do it?' I say.

'He couldn't. Not that it mattered. By now, Mouldy's a whimpering wreck. I put me hand in the middle of his chest. I tell him, "This is for Davie and his mate." '

'For Davie and his mate?' I gasp.

'Aye, Davie. Of course. Then I shove, and over he goes like a little kitten. A bump, a yell, a crash. Bye-bye, Mouldy.'

He smiles at my silence. I close my eyes. I want to think nothing, to feel nothing.

'And me and Clay,' says Stephen. 'We wander back here in time for morning.'

He laughs.

'We'll train him up, eh? Destroy!'

I open my eyes. There's another angel in Clay's fist. He crushes it and the fragments and dust crumble over me.

'See?' says Stephen. 'He'll soon get the idea. Destroy, Clay! Hahaha!'

Forty-Five

The brilliance in the sky has gone. The distinction between the shaft of light and the shadowy corners is fading. I stand with Clay in a kind of twilight. He holds me. I lean on this impossible creature. I feel the cold strength in him and I want to stay here with him. I don't want to go out into the cold outside, into the cold truth of Mouldy's death and of my part in it. I don't want to go back into the truth of parents and policemen and priests. It's so alien out there. Geordie, Maria, Prat Parker, they're like characters in a story, beings from another world.

Stephen smiles. He passes his hand before my eyes. He knows what's going on inside.

'It used to be so easy, Davie, didn't it?' he says. 'And now such weird things has come to pass. And mebbe the weirdest thing of all is this – the only one that understands you now is me, Stephen Rose.'

He pats my shoulder, pats Clay.

'Don't let it bother you,' he says. 'Howay, let's go inside. Let's have some jam and bread and settle you down before you go back home again. Clay, lie down and do nowt else till me and Davie tell you.'

Clay unfolds his arms from me. He lies flat on the floor alongside the shed wall. I crouch beside him, touch him. Nothing in him. He's nothing but clay in the figure of a man.

We leave the shed and walk through the channel in the long grass towards Crazy's kitchen. Stephen ushers me inside. He goes into the other room. I hear his words: 'Five, four, three, two, one, wake up, Mary!' and soon she's with him in the doorway.

'It's the good altar boy,' says Stephen.

'Oh, aye,' says Mary. 'Would you like some jam and bread?'

I don't reply. She hacks at a loaf for a moment.

'I must have fell asleep again,' she says. 'So much sleeping and waking these days, I cannot hardly tell what's going on.'

'You need your rest, Aunty Mary,' says Stephen.

'That's true,' she answers. 'And in sleep the angels come with all their messages and tales, so mebbe it's a blessing.'

She hacks again.

'You ever see an angel, son?' she says.

I shake my head.

'You ever see a monster?'

I shake my head.

'I seen one in——' she says.

'Aunty Mary!' says Stephen.

'Aye, son?'

'I telt you. There's no monsters.'

'No monsters?'

He passes his hand before her eyes.

'There's no bliddy monsters,' he says. 'Is there?'

'Is there what?' she says.

'Is there any monsters, Aunty Mary?'

She giggles.

'Monsters?' she says. 'Course there's no monsters.'

She spreads margarine then jam on thick slices of bread.

'But there is angels,' she says.

'Aye,' says Stephen. 'There is angels.'

'And they're lovely.'

'Aye. They're lovely.'

She pours tea for me, shoves jam and bread at me.

'Eat,' she says. 'Eat and drink.'

I cannot.

'You must,' she tells me. 'This is the good food of the Lord.'

She watches as I nibble at a crust, then stretches across and rests two fingers on my brow. Stephen laughs and shoves her hand away from me, but for the moment that her cold dry fingertips rest upon my skin, I feel the comfort in them. I look into her crazy eyes and try to see through the craziness to what might lie behind. She blinks.

'Aunty Mary!' commands Stephen.

She stops. I stand up. Stephen guides me out.

'You got to act like everything is normal,' he says as we stand at the door. 'We got great things to do together, you and me and Clay.' He passes his hand before my eyes.

'You got to keep thinking of him,' he says. 'Keep him existing in your mind. Only then can he keep existing in the world. And stay calm.'

I'm more than calm. I'm dead still, stupefied. It's like all strength has drained away from me.

'Come back tomorrow, Davie,' he says.

He opens the door. I breathe the outside air. I step out into the world again and very soon I see Maria.

Forty-Six

By now it's like I've stopped being me. It's like I've got no will, no purpose, like something's moving me through the world, like every footstep is controlled by something far beyond me. The sparrowhawk's wheeling in the white sky over Braddock's Garden. Trees are black etches, houses are looming walls. The by-pass is a distant groaning engine. Maria's on a bench, like something not alive, like a pretty white-faced puppet left there on the bright-green wooden slats above the bright-green blades of grass. I'm passing her by when she rises from the bench. Her mouth opens and some words come out but I don't know what they are. She grabs my shoulder and tugs at me. Her white face looms close.

'What's happening?' she hisses.

I try to speak but nothing comes out.

She shakes me. She says my name.

'All that stuff they say about you and Stephen Rose,' she says. 'I know it's rubbish. But I know there's something more, Davie.'

I grunt, stutter, try to speak.

'I'll believe anything, Davie. Tell me.'

'Clay lives,' I say at last.

I take her hands.

'What do you mean?' she says.

I grip her hands.

'Clay lives,' I stammer. 'Clay moves. We made him, Maria.'

'Him?'

'Him. And he . . .'

'He what, Davie?'

I peer into her trusting eyes.

'Nothing,' I whisper.

'Can't tell you,' I whisper.

'Got to go,' I whisper.

I drop her hands. I move away. She catches me up. She kisses me.

'You can tell me anything,' she says. 'I'll believe anything.'

She lets me go. Sometimes I hear her behind me as I walk. I move on through the familiar streets and lanes, and with every footstep they become more strange to me.

Forty-Seven

And at home they watch me enter, and my mother says I'm late and I lower my head and tell her I'm sorry. And my father looks out through the window and he sees a girl out there and he says, 'Aha! So that's the reason!' And they both smile. And I do, too. And the girl departs. And we eat a meal together and they do not question me too much, and when they do I am able to grunt replies that appear to satisfy them. And I go to my room and open a book and place it on a table below my eyes and I stare into it but see nowt in it and there is nowt in my mind and the evening passes by and darkness comes on and I am called down to meet with my parents again and we drink warm liquids and say our good nights and I am returned to my room and I lie on my bed and the nowtness deepens and the darkness deepens, and I am truly not myself, I am truly gone, I have disappeared from the world, no thoughts

no feelings no sensations no dreams, just nowt nowt
nowt nowt, and then at last from all the nowtness
comes the voice.

Master. I am here.

Forty-Eight

There he is, down below the streetlight, huge round face turned up to me, arms hanging at his side, great feet planted on the pavement.

'Clay,' I whisper to myself.

I am here, Master.

I find that I'm still dressed. I leave the house. I go to him. His head turns like a clockwork thing to follow my approach. There's no expression on his face or in his words.

'Clay,' I whisper.

Command me, Master.

I stare. What could *I* command?

'Just follow me,' I say.

I lead him from the single streetlight. He plods beside me like a massive faithful pet. We walk in silence, deep in gloom, then I find my voice, a simple stupid voice.

'This is Felling,' I say as we start to pass the houses and their gardens, as I lead him through my world. 'This is the town I come from. This is where I live.'

We walk uphill, towards the top of town, through Chilside Road, Rectory Road, Crowhall Lane, up Felling Bank.

Not a soul to be seen. Hardly a light. The moon is dim behind a veil of clouds. I name names as we walk.

'The Hagans live in there. Douggie's in my class at school. His sister's Catherine. That's the Wilsons' house. Mr Pew the parkie lives upstairs in that one. Vincent Grant, Elizabeth Grant, Aloysious Thomas Grant. The Flynns. The Mintos. The Dougalls. The Carrs.'

He doesn't respond. I keep looking at him. I keep telling myself he isn't there, he can't be there. But he is there, and he's walking at my side. I allow my hand to brush against him, to assure myself that he is there. When I stop talking, I hear him again.

I am here, Master. Command me, Master.

'The Kinkaids that live here have got a dog called Buster and a cat called Kit. The Potters go to Crimdon Dene in their caravan each August. Mrs Penberthy once met Elvis Presley. The Turners lost a son to diphtheria. Teresa Duffy has a fragment of the one true cross.'

Once or twice a car passes by but we stand dead still

in shadow and they don't seem to see and then we move again.

I point different directions into the night.

'The baths is that way. Brian Phelps practises diving there. He's been in the Olympics. Over there's where we play football. We support Newcastle. They're not that good but they're the best. The school is just beyond it. School's where we learn about the world and us and where we try to find out what we think and what we can imagine and create. Prat Parker is a prat but he's OK. Me granda's allotment's that way. His tomatoes are lovely. Me grandma turns them into chutney.'

I turn to face him.

'Are you listening?' I ask him.

He stares straight back at me.

'Are you thinking?' I say.

His eyes are dark, like sycamore-seed-shaped gaps in the clay that nothing enters and nothing leaves.

'Where did *you* come from, Clay?'

I am here, Master. Command me.

I lead him on. Higher up, there are many lights on in Queen Elizabeth Hospital. We don't approach. An ambulance turns in at the hospital gate.

'This is the hospital, Clay. It's where lots of us are born. Where we come into the world.'

His eyes swivel to me again.

'We start as nothing,' I say. 'Then we appear inside our mothers, then we leave our mothers and come into the world.'

A siren starts to blare. Another ambulance appears.

'It's also where lots of us leave the world,' I tell him. I ponder what I'm saying. 'Or where some part of us leaves the world,' I say. I think again.

I am here, Master. Command me.

'Just follow me,' I say.

We turn downhill again. I name the names. The Post Office. The Black Horse. Windy Nook Club. Lasky's pig farm over that way. The chip shop. George Lang the bookie's shop. Pearson's, where you get beautiful boiled ham, brown ale, butter cut from in a barrel. Mays' Fashion's with its mad apostrophes. The hill drops steeply to the square. A drunk totters past us, lifts his cap, staggers.

'Evening, boy and great big bliddy giant,' he says, and he giggles and stumbles and belches and totters on.

'That's Geordie's Uncle Joe,' I say. 'But he'll remember nowt.'

We pass Dragone's coffee shop. I tell him that we all go there, young and old, that people whisper secrets and tell tall tales and learn to smoke and fall in love in there. And I tell him that the ice cream is the best and that I first found out the deliciousness of Horlicks in there. And I lead him on and I show him the Corona Cinema and the Palais de Dans and the shops that line the High Street and the abundance of things that fill the windows there and I see Clay and myself reflected in the glass and I halt and I feel that my heart will stop with the astonishment of it.

'Do you see, Clay?' I whisper. 'There's me, there's you. We're together in the world.'

We move closer to the window. We stand in the middle of the street. We face ourselves looking back at ourselves. I wave. 'Raise your hand,' I say, and Clay raises his hand as if he's waving, too. Then I lead him on. I show him the closed gates of Howie's junkyard, the alleyway to my uncle's printing shop. I tell him about Myers' pies and pork sandwiches and about the gossiping groups and the playing kids that fill the street by day. And then St Patrick's Church is looming over us.

'That's where God is,' I tell him. 'Or where we think he is. Or he's everywhere, but this is where he is most of all, where we can get closest to him. Or something like that.'

The steeple appears to be toppling below the drifting clouds. I watch it toppling but of course it's an illusion and it doesn't fall.

'God made everything,' I said. 'And he sees everything, and knows everything.'

I am here, Master. Command me.

I sigh.

'Or maybe he's stopped seeing us and knowing us,' I say. 'What do *you* think, Clay?'

Nothing, of course.

I lean so close to him.

'Do *you* believe in God, Clay?'

No answer, of course.

'Did God make you?' I ask.

Silence, of course.

We stand together, and each of us is silent, and dark, and purposeless.

'What can I do with you?' I sigh.

No answer again. And we stand there in silence for minute after minute after minute, and Clay becomes dead still.

'Are you gone, Clay?' I whisper, and I know that part of me, most of me, wishes that he has gone, that he is nothing but a lifeless lump of earth again, that he will never come back again. I touch him. Clay cold.

'Clay?' I whisper.

And I feel the life trickling back into him.

'Come along,' I sigh. 'Now I'll show you where we go when we are gone.'

248

Forty-Nine

He has to stoop to enter through the gate. The bats are out. A pair of owls are hunting, hooting. The veil of clouds is clearing below the moon. Clay's feet rasp on the gravel path as we walk deeper in.

'This is the graveyard,' I say. 'Thousands of the dead are buried here. Many of my family are here. My ancestors.'

I show the ancient leaning graves. I show the Braddock graves.

Once again, I find I'm naming names. I crouch close to the earth, and read by the moonlight the names carved into the stones.

'Elizabeth Grace McCracken,' I say. 'Born 1789. Taken into Glory 1878. Beloved wife of . . . Beloved mother of . . . William Edward Carr. Georgina Fay . . .'

I want to explain, to make him understand, even though I know he can't understand, that the things I say must be beyond him.

'We're brought here when life has gone from us,' I say. 'When we're nothing but a body, we're put into the earth.'

He turns the empty channels of his eyes to me.

Command me, Master.

'Dust to dust,' I say, and I realise that the things I say, the things that we all say, are beyond me, too.

I move on. I take him past the newer graves. I continue naming names as we go. Soon we're near the fence that separates the graveyard from the by-pass. There's a newly-dug grave, with a few boards across the opening, and a mound of earth beside it. I tug away a board. I peer down into the dark.

'This is the earth, Clay. This is what we start from and where we end.'

I take a handful of earth. I roll it into a ball. I throw it down into the dark.

'Earth to earth,' I say. 'Clay to clay.'

We stand together at the grave's edge.

'This is where Martin Mould will go,' I say.

Command me, Master.

I throw another handful of earth into the earth. I turn away, and he follows.

'Now we must go back to the garden,' I say.

Fifty

There's a police sign, readable by moonlight: NO UNAUTHORISED PERSONS MAY ENTER. A skull and crossbones, glaring white. DANGER OF DEATH.

I lead Clay past them and through the ruined gates.

'This is the oldest place in Felling,' I tell him as we push through the hawthorn, as we head for the quarry.

'This is where you started,' I say. 'Do you remember?'

I point up to the quarry's rim.

'That's where Mouldy fell. You were with Stephen Rose. Do you remember?'

We come to the clay pond. I take out a handful of clay.

'This is you,' I tell him.

I spread a handful of it on his chest. It starts to dry on him, becoming him. He pays no attention.

I am here, Master. Command me.

I take out another handful. I form it to a tiny human shape.

'Live,' I whisper, and though it stays dead still, I imagine life squirming in it. Could Stephen and I fill the garden with such creatures? Could we populate a whole new world? For a moment I have a vision of our stubby little creatures running through the undergrowth. I see them with the frogs and the snake beneath the sparrowhawk wheeling high above. I see them, moving out of the garden and into the world. I shudder, and cast the vision from me, and I allow the handful of clay to fall back with a splash into the pond.

'It wasn't long ago,' I say. 'You lay there on the ground. We were beside you, Stephen Rose and I. You were so beautiful. We made you and we begged you to live and prayed for you to live. I wanted to believe that life could enter you just like it departs the dead. I wanted to believe that dust to dust might mean death to life just as it means life to death. But you don't understand me, do you? This is all beyond you, just like it's all beyond me.'

I sigh at the uselessness of my words.

'I'm just a boy,' I say. 'You're just a lump of clay. I can't do this. I want nowt to do with you and nowt to do with Stephen bliddy Rose!'

I look into the sky. The moon is sliding over us. The

night is passing by. I find myself thinking of Geordie, laughing and joking and swaggering around the streets with him. I think of us setting up traps in the quarry. I think of battling with Skinner and Poke. I think of Prat Parker catching jelly babies in the air. I think of Maria, her face, her skin, her voice, her lips against my lips.

'I've got me own bliddy life to live!' I say.

Command me, Master.

'I don't want a great big stupid living lump of clay!'

Command me, Master.

I try to look deep into his sycamore eyes.

'I want you to lie down, Clay,' I murmur. 'You've been walking all night. You must be tired. Lie down.'

There's no response.

'Do it, Clay.'

I take his arm, tug it gently downwards, towards the earth.

'Please, Clay.'

Master.

'Lie down.' I say it more loudly. 'Lie down. Be still!'

And he obeys. He sits on the ground and slowly turns his face to me.

'That's right,' I say. 'Good Clay.'

Master. My master.

'Now lie down properly.'

I shove his shoulder gently. He resists for a moment, then he lies down.

'Well done,' I whisper. 'Now sleep. Sleep.'

He lies there, so still.

'We all do it,' I tell him. 'We close our eyes and the darkness and nowtness come into us. Sleep. Sleep.'

I hear his voice inside me, distant and diminishing and so faint.

Master . . . Oh, Master.

I crouch beside him.

'Relax,' I say. 'Be still. Let the darkness come into you.' I lean so close. I breathe the words so softly into his ear. 'Goodbye, Clay.'

Master. Oh, Master.

'Die, Clay. Please die.'

And I feel the spirit leaving him. I feel him retreat to the very edge of existence. But suddenly there are footsteps in the garden, coming closer.

Fifty-One

Stephen Rose, gentle at first. He stands there by the clay pond, hands on his hips.

'What you doing, Davie?'

'Nowt.'

'Nowt?'

'Nowt.'

'What you doing with Clay?'

'He come to me. He found me. We been walking.'

'*Walking?*'

'Aye. Round Felling.'

'Hell's teeth, Davie.'

'Nobody seen us.'

He comes a little closer.

'And what you doing now?' he says.

'Nowt. Just being with him.'

'Ahhh, that's nice. Come here, Clay. Clay, get up and come to your master.'

'Stay,' I whisper.

I rest my hand on Clay's brow. He's so still. He's almost gone. There's almost nothing in him.

'Looks like I came just at the right time, Davie,' says Stephen.

'Does it?'

'Aye. Looks like you were doing wicked things out here, Davie.'

'Aye?'

'Aye. I think you were doing away with our creation, Davie.'

His eyes glitter like stars in the deep black shadows of his face.

'Am I right, Davie?' he says.

'I don't reply. He comes closer, stares down at our creature.

'Clay,' he says. 'Clay! Move!'

He shoves Clay with his foot. 'Clay! Move!' And Clay stirs, and life moves in him again, and Stephen smiles.

'See, Davie? You haven't got the strength to finish him off properly. Now get up, Clay. Live!' He shoves Clay with his foot again. 'Come to your master.'

'No,' I say. 'It isn't right!'

'Get up, monster!'

Clay raises himself. He rolls over, gets on to his hands

and knees. I stand beside him. I try to hold him. There's no voice in him. He gets up slowly, clumsily.

'Leave him alone! Can you not feel how scared he is?'

'Ahhh, that's nice,' says Stephen. 'Davie's worried about you, Clay. Get *up*, monster!'

Clay kneels, he stands.

'He's in bliddy pain, Stephen!'

Clay stands at Stephen's side. Stephen leans through the dark that lies between us.

'You think I care how scared he is? You think I'm bothered about his pain? Mebbe this is how to make a proper monster, Davie. Drag him back and forward between life and death. Make him suffer, make him bliddy terrified.' He grins. 'Then give him a job to do.'

He stands tall, speaks softly into Clay's ear. He watches me while he speaks.

'Clay,' he says. 'This is Davie. This is the one that helped to make you. This is the one that should have loved you and looked after you. But this Davie is a devil. He was putting an end to you, Clay. He was killing you. What do you think about that?'

And they watch me, the boy and the monster, and they seem to be in such harmony – the monster dead still, the boy's voice so soft and his smile so sweet as he whispers his commands.

'Now, Clay,' says Stephen. 'I want you to destroy this devil called Davie. I want you to kill.'

The monster steps towards me. Its hands reach out to me.

Stephen's teeth are bared. Saliva's dripping from them. 'Kill!' he snarls. 'Kill, Clay! Kill!'

I'm backing away with my arms raised.

'No, Clay!' I say. 'Stop, Clay!'

But he's got me by the throat.

'Please, Clay. No! No!'

His hands are tightening on me. I can't speak. I can hardly breathe.

'Yes!' says Stephen. He comes closer. 'Do it, Clay. Now, Clay!'

I look up into Clay's sycamore eyes. And now his own words are inside me, and they're so frail, so filled with pain.

Oh, Master. Oh, Master . . .

His hands start to relax.

'Clay,' I gasp. 'Please let me go.'

And he can't go on. His hands fall away from me. He slumps to his knees, and his head hangs towards the earth.

Stephen spits.

'Pathetic,' he whispers. 'There's too much of the Davie in you, Clay.'

I gather my strength, my breath.

'So come on,' I say to him. 'Finish me like you finished Mouldy.'

He reaches towards me and moves his hand across my eyes. I shove it away.

'Come on,' I tell him. 'Try it, Stephen.'

We circle each other, then we jump.

Fifty-Two

We grab each other's throats. He nuts me, nuts me again. I punch him under the ribs and we fall apart and curse and growl and spit and glare.

'You,' he says. 'You were always wrong. Should've known it from the start. Too weak, too stupid, too young.'

We fight again. I shove his face into the ground. He squirms away.

'I'll do it on me own next time,' he says. He spits saliva, snot and blood. 'I'll make a monster filled with evil and nowt else.'

We fight again. We fall apart. I'm trembling with the effort of it.

'You couldn't do it without me,' I say.

'Could I not? I can do bliddy anything, Davie. You just held me back.'

I swing a fist. It misses him. He catches it, lunges at it,

bites it, chews it. I shove his head away with my other hand. We fight again, collapse again.

'Mebbe you were sent to help me find the way,' he says. He laughs. 'You've been me servant, Davie. Ha! Now it's time to leave you behind.'

We crouch like animals, on all fours. We glare at each other through the night.

'There's a purpose for me,' he says. 'I won't find it in simple stupid ordinary Felling with simple stupid ordinary you.'

'Find it somewhere else, then.'

'I will.' He wipes his face with his sleeve. 'But before I go, I'll tell you about me mother, and me father. Just so you know a little bit more of what Stephen Rose can do.'

I watch him and wait. He grins. He knows I want to know.

'Your mother . . .' I say.

'Is a bag,' he says. 'Is a bitch.'

'She's ill.'

'She's barmy.'

'She needs you.'

'I spit on her,' he says. 'Pah!'

And he spits.

'Here's the truth about me mother,' he says. 'She never wanted me. She never even expected me. Listen to this – she telt me that her and me stupid dad never done nowt together for two years before I was born. She telt me there was just a month to go before she looked down at her belly and said, "Hell's teeth, there's a bliddy bairn in there!" '

'That can't be true.'

'Mebbe not in your world, Davie. But in mine . . .'

'It can't be.'

'Ha! And then she started seeing what it was that'd slithered out of her and she wanted it gone again. Too late. It was that that sent her barmy. That, and being at the table when I killed me dad.'

He grins. He dares to crawl closer. His face is almost pressing against mine. I feel his breath on me.

'Aye, Davie. When I killed him. Killed him! Killed him as sure as if I'd stuck a knife straight into his heart. Remember what I telt you last time? He was stuffing steak and kidney pud into his stupid face, and she was goggling at the stupid telly and *Look North*? Aye, that was true enough. A nice little ordinary family scene. But I was staring at his face in horror, because he was ugly and horrible and I was sick of him, and inside I start going, "Die, you cretin. Die." And he keeps on stuffing and stuffing, and I start letting the words slip out, dead soft at first, "Die, you cretin. Die." And I let them get louder and he hears them and stares across his pud and she turns her stupid face round from *Look North*. "Aye," I tell them. "I'm telling him to die," and their faces go all shocked, and she comes for me, but I say it loud, "Die, you cretin, die," and then he does his gagging and his gurgling and his tumble to the floor.'

He grins again.

'Who'd believe it?' he whispers. 'Who'd believe there's a son that's wicked enough to kill his dad? Why, it's nearly as daft as believing in a god and angels. It's nearly as daft as believing in a walking lump of clay.'

I'm silent. I have no answers.

'I'm not like you, Davie,' he whispers. 'I come out of the darkness and the nowtness and I was sent here by something and there is a purpose to me. I'm different from you. I spit on you.'

And he spits in my face, and I go at him and we fight again, and I press him to the ground, punch him, kneel on his shoulders. I pick a rock up from the ground. I lift it high. And for a moment, he stops struggling.

'Aye,' he whispers. 'Do it, Davie. Smash me face in. I'm waiting. Go on, put an end to me.'

I can't move.

'Do it!' he says. 'Mebbe it'll be better for you and your world if you get rid of me now.'

He waits. I feel the rock in my hand. I know it could

break his skull. But there's no way I could do it. I let it fall.

'That's my Davie,' says Stephen. 'You can't finish me, so just let me go.'

I roll off him. I see Clay crawling on all fours away from us into the undergrowth.

'Clay!' I call.

'Clay!' echoes Stephen, in a high girly mocking voice.

He gets up, wipes the dirt off himself.

'It's strange,' says Stephen. 'I've stopped believing in both of you now. You were both just try-outs. You were both just steps on me way.'

Clay crawls further into the darkness, goes out of sight.

Stephen's voice follows him.

'Die, Clay,' he breathes. 'Be still, Clay.'

I catch my breath. Stephen smiles at me.

'It's what you wanted, isn't it?' he says. 'Die, Clay. Be still, Clay.' He grins. 'Die, you cretin. Die.'

He passes his hands before my eyes.

'You think you're so good, don't you?' he says. 'You, that butchered a dog. You, that wanted Mouldy dead. You, that helped to make the thing that helped to kill Mouldy. You, that was about to kill Clay. Well, there's goodness for you. There's an ordinary life for you.'

I gaze into the darkness of his eyes.

265

'And here's a thought for you to ponder in your ordinary life,' he whispers. 'If you'd not run back like a baby to your bed that night, your Mr Mouldy could be with us still.'

He smiles once more, then passes his hands before my eyes again.

'It's over,' he whispers. 'Go back to being a simple stupid soul, Davie.'

Then he's gone, and there's just me, alone in the quarry, in the night.

Fifty-Three

I search for Clay. I whisper his name. I crawl on all
fours through the undergrowth. I'm about to give up
when I stumble across him. I call his name, but he's
dead and gone. I try to pray for him, but what god can
I pray to? What god would recognise Clay? It starts to
rain as I crouch over him. The water runs across his
skin, already carrying him back into the earth. I open
him up and search with my fingers in the depths of
him. I find the locket, take it out, and close him up
again. The rain intensifies.

'Goodbye, Clay,' I say.

I hold my face up to the rain. I let it wash the mud
and blood and tears away. Then I hurry home. It's
already turning light. Miserable steel-grey clouds hang
over Felling. The rain drums down. I slip into the
house. I stand for a moment on the landing. I hear my
parents' breathing as they sleep. I open their door and

look in on them. I wait for them to wake and to see me there. 'I'm here,' I whisper, but they hardly stir. I feel like Clay – stiff, heavy, dull – like I'm something at the very edge of life. I feel that I could be washed away, that I could disappear. 'I'm here,' I whisper more loudly. There's no response. Are they dreaming me as I stand there, as I close their door, as I leave them? I go to my room. I hide my clothes. I hide the locket. I look out into the endless night. Who thinks all this? Who believes all this? Who dreams all this? Then nowtness overcomes me, and I sleep.

Four

Fifty-Four

Time moves forward, so we're told. Day leads to night leads to day leads to night. Past, present, future. Child, teenager, adult. Birth, life, death. But sometimes time gets stuck. We can't move on.

After the final night in Braddock's Garden, Stephen Rose wasn't seen again. But the memories kept coming back at me. They kept on happening in my thoughts and dreams, in a kind of endless present. I thought I caught glimpses of Stephen in the crowds on the High Street or in Felling Square. I thought I saw him in the shadows of the graveyard or Holly Hill Park, or beyond the boarded-up gates of Braddock's Garden. But when I looked more closely, I was wrong. It was somebody who looked like him, or it was a shifting shadow, or a cat or a bird or a dog, or just a figment.

In my dreams, Clay stirred again, started to move for the first time again. Stephen kept on whispering in my ear, his hands kept moving across my eyes. Mouldy kept on falling and falling and falling to his doom. I wanted it all to be finished. But it wouldn't leave me, and I couldn't forget, and I became a trapped, stupid, useless thing.

The day after the final night, Crazy Mary came knocking at our door. She was wild-eyed, wild-haired, with tartan slippers and an ancient overcoat on. 'Where's my boy?' she whispered at me. 'You're his friend. Where's he gone?' I looked at Mam and spread my hands as if to ask her, 'What's the crazy woman on about?' Mam brought her in, she stroked her arm, she tried to calm her down. But Mary kept on babbling: her boy had gone to bed at night, he'd disappeared in the morning. She clapped her hand across her mouth. 'I'm not still sleeping, am I?' she said. 'There really was a boy? His name was Stephen Rose? And he was sent to me?' Yes, we told her. Yes. 'Then where's he gone?' she asked me. 'You're his friend. What's become of him?' I kept on telling her I didn't know. I kept on telling her I wasn't his proper friend. I glared at Mam: how was I supposed to know? In the end, they prayed together, and Mam looked over Mary's shoulder and told me to call the police.

And Sergeant Fox and PC Ground came, and they filled the room, with their massive shoulders and their badges and helmets and their shiny boots. They sat down this time, and swigged tea.

'He's a good pal of yours,' said Sergeant Fox.

'Not good,' I said.

'Right. Not good. And the last time you saw him was . . .'

He licked his pencil and watched me while my mind raced.

'Couple of days back,' I said. 'I went to Crazy . . . to Miss Doonan's house.'

'And what did you do and what did you talk about?'

'We were in the shed. He showed me his sculptures. Then Miss Doonan made tea for us. Then I came home.'

'And did he seem upset in any way? And did he talk about going off somewhere?'

'No. No.'

'That's good.'

He tapped his head and thought.

'It's been a strange week for you, son.'

'Strange?' I said.

'One lad dying. Now another disappearing.'

I lowered my eyes.

'Yes,' I murmured.

'It can't be easy for you, but don't worry. It's easy to disappear. It's staying disappeared that's the hardest trick.'

'We're on the trail,' said PC Ground.

'Do you think they're related in any way?' said Sergeant Fox.

'Who?' I said.

'The dead and the disappeared, son. Do you know of any links?'

He watched me while I thought. I saw Mouldy's eyes, glaring through the letter box. I felt Stephen's kiss on my cheek.

'Did Stephen Rose know Martin Mould?' said Sergeant Fox.

'He kept away from him,' I said.

'Did they ever meet?'

I saw Mouldy teetering on the quarry edge. I saw Stephen's outspread hand on Mouldy's chest.

'No,' I said. 'I don't know. I don't think so.'

'They were very different types,' said Dad.

'Very different types,' said Sergeant Fox as he wrote. 'Good.' He looked me in the eye. 'Now, then, young man. We'll need you to tell us everything you know about Stephen Rose.'

'Everything?'

'Everything. We'll need to know what he's like deep inside. Like, what're his true interests? His . . . passions.'

'What drives him?' said PC Ground. 'And what is it

out there in the world that's tempted him away from Felling and Miss Doonan's tender care.'

The sergeant waited, wide-eyed, pencil poised.

I stared back at him. I searched for words.

'I know, son,' said the sergeant. 'It's a very difficult question.'

'Every one of us is a puzzle,' said PC Ground.

'An enigma,' said the sergeant. 'That's what this job teaches us. Aye, PC Ground?'

'Aye,' said PC Ground.

'Of course,' said the sergeant. 'We'll be looking into the weird tales that came with him.'

'Aye,' said PC Ground. 'The legends, as it were.' He leaned towards me with his brows furrowed. 'Tell us, son,' he said. 'Did you ever see anything strange in him.'

'Strange?'

'You saw nowt . . .'

I watched them, their waiting eyes, the pencils in their hands. How could I tell them of the strangeness that I'd seen? How could it be scribbled into a notebook?

'I saw nowt,' I said. 'Stephen Rose is just a kid, just like me. Just like all us kids.'

Sergeant Fox scribbled that down.

'He's nowt special,' I said. 'But his dad died, and his

mam lost her mind, and he was sent all alone to Felling, and he doesn't fit in. That's all.'

'That's very perceptive, son,' said the sergeant.

'He's good at sculpture,' I said. 'He makes little statues. They're brilliant. It's almost like they're alive.'

'Alive?' said Sergeant Fox. 'Is that right, now?'

'Aye,' I said. 'He's an artist.'

'With a troubled past and a troubled mind,' said Mam.

'An artist with a troubled mind,' said Sergeant Fox as he scribbled. 'I like that.' He stabbed a full stop on to the page then he shook his head and looked at us. 'There but for the grace of God, eh?'

We led them to the door. They told us not to worry. They said they'd find our Stephen and bring him home to us again.

Fifty-Five

The next Saturday, I went to Mouldy's funeral. I stood under the graveyard trees and watched from a distance. A few other Felling folk were scattered around. The mourners came in a Ford Zephyr and a Transit van. His mam stood weeping into her hands. There were a few bulky relatives in black, and a vicar droning just about the same words as Father O'Mahoney would say. Mouldy's coffin was lowered into the grave that I'd stood beside with Clay. It disappeared from sight, then flowers and soil and water were thrown in after it. I tried to say a prayer for Mouldy, then I found Geordie at my side.

'D'you think he's watching us?' he said.

'Who?'

'Mouldy, man. From the afterlife.'

I shook my head, looked around, half-expecting to see Stephen Rose watching from the shadows or from beyond the graveyard gate.

'Even if he is,' I said, 'he couldn't do nowt now.'

'Except haunt us,' Geordie said.

We watched the mourners. We were silent and scared for a while.

'Mebbe Mouldy's ghost'll start to walk,' said Geordie. 'Mebbe kids'll start to see a great big bliddy monster by the light of the moon in Braddock's Garden.' He tried to laugh. 'I'm going to scare my kids with that one once they're here.'

The mourners dispersed. The vicar helped Mrs Mould back to the car. I shuddered. I imagined myself lying silent and still in the earth while my family walked away from me.

'Still no sign of Stephen Rose, then?' said Geordie.

I shook my head.

'Good riddance, eh?' he said. 'Bliddy loony.'

'Aye,' I said.

We saw Skinner and Poke coming through the trees towards us.

'Aye, aye, lads,' said Geordie.

'How do,' said Poke.

'Poor bugger, eh?' said Skinner, nodding towards the grave.

'Aye,' we all said.

We avoided each other's eyes. We didn't dare speak our fright.

'He did have a good side to him,' said Skinner.

'Aye,' we said.

'In fact,' said Geordie, 'you could say he was a very nice young man.'

We stifled our laughs.

'He'll be sorely missed,' said Poke.

And we relaxed.

'Do you want to make peace?' said Skinner.

'Aye,' said Geordie.

'OK,' said Poke.

They all shook hands. I shook hands as well.

'That's done, then,' said Skinner. 'No more battling.'

'That's right, you Pelaw Proddy gits,' said Geordie.

'You Felling Catholic prats,' said Poke.

We all pretended to face up to each other, like we were going to start to fight, but we just started giggling.

'I'm going up to see me Windy Nook mates,' said Geordie. 'Mebbe we'll ploat some Springwellers. You want to come?'

'Aye,' said Skinner and Poke.

They all looked at me.

'No,' I said. I shrugged. 'I cannot,' I said.

They looked at the grave a last time, then they walked away. I soon followed them. I couldn't stop thinking of the dead laid out beneath my feet, until I found Maria waiting at the graveyard gate. We walked together. She told me again that I could tell her anything, but I said I didn't know where to start, I didn't know how to make her believe. We walked all afternoon. We kissed beneath the trees in Holly Hill Park, and as we kissed I began to forget Stephen Rose and Mouldy. It was like I almost started to disappear, until the parkie Mr Pew was yelling at us: 'Hoy! You two! Sling your blinking hook!' And we walked on hand in hand, and it was like Maria was some kind of guardian, sent to stop me sinking even further into gloom.

Fifty-Six

At dusk, I said I should go to confession. We went into St Patrick's. I knelt in the dark confessional. I could see Father O'Mahoney's face through the grille. I didn't try to disguise my voice.

'Bless me, Father,' I said, 'for I have sinned.'

He waited. I was silent.

'Go on, my son,' he said. 'What must you confess?'

I imagined the words coming out of my mouth: *I stole the body and blood of Christ, I killed a dog, I created a creature, the creature helped to murder Martin Mould, I helped to kill the creature. I lied to my parents and held back evidence from the police. I . . .*

'Well?' he murmured, but still I couldn't speak. We looked at each other through the grille.

'It's you, Davie,' he said.

'Yes, Father.'

'It is more than calling people Fishface, I suspect.'

'Yes, but you wouldn't believe me, Father.'

'I've heard everything in here. You can tell me anything. I'm just a channel for your words. It is between you and God.'

'I don't know if there is a God, Father.'

'Ha!'

'I think there may once have been a God, but he got sick of us and he left us.'

'I see that adolescence is truly upon you. This is not a place for discussion. Just confess, do your penance, be done with it. Other penitents are waiting outside.'

'I hated a person and wished for his death,' I murmured.

'Ah. That is indeed a sin. And are you sorry for it?'

'Yes. But the death happened.'

'Ah. So it weighs on your heart.'

'Yes. The person was Martin Mould, Father.'

'The boy who fell.'

'Yes, the boy who fell.'

'You must not blame yourself.'

I was silent.

'You must not,' he said again. 'Each of us has intentions and desires that we must curb. Your wish was indeed a sin. But there is a gap between sinful wishes and sinful deeds.'

Our eyes met through the grille.

'You understand, Davie,' he said. 'Had you pushed him, it would be different. I take it you did not push him.'

'No, Father.'

'That's grand. What else must you confess?'

I searched for words.

'Do you believe in evil, Father?'

'Davie, I've told you, this is not the place.'

'Do you, Father?'

'I believe in weakness, Davie. I believe we can be led astray. I have spent many hours in this box. I have heard of a million awful thoughts, a million awful acts. We can be petty little creatures with petty little wickednesses. We gain strength and goodness by turning our hearts to God.'

'But if you believe in God and goodness, should you not believe in the devil and evil?'

'Yes, but I am an optimist, Davie. I believe that God and goodness have the upper hand.'

'But there *is* evil?'

'You tell me that you doubt the existence of God, but you want me to tell you to believe in evil?'

'Please, Father.'

He sighed in exasperation.

'Yes,' he said. 'I do think there is evil. But it is very rare. It is as rare as true goodness. And just as true goodness produces rare saints, true evil produces rare monsters. The rest of us are semi-good, semi-bad, and we live our lives in a kind of half-happy, half-sad daze. We might hope that one sunny morning we find ourselves in the presence of a saint. And we must pray very hard that we do not encounter the monster. Now, we've discussed enough. Tell me another sin. There are others waiting.'

I said nothing.

'Davie! Speak now. Or I'll throw you out.'

'Stephen Rose,' I whispered.

'Stephen Rose?'

'You were supposed to look out for him, Father.'

I saw the frown cross his face.

'Yes,' he said. He looked sternly through the grille, then he sighed, and spoke softly, as if in confession himself. 'I'm troubled by what has occurred, Davie. I did look out for him. But my flock is large. And I thought that the influence of lads like yourself and George . . .' His voice trailed off. 'They'll find him,' he said. 'They'll bring him home again. We'll make a better job of it next time.'

'What was he, Father?'

'Ha. Just a boy, a little older than yourself. A boy with problems. There but for the grace of God. But just an ordinary boy. And now, another sin.'

I searched my thoughts.

I imagined: *I stole the body and blood of Christ. I . . .*

'I stole a cigarette from my dad,' I said.

'Oh, Davie. Yet again? And smoked it?'

'Yes, Father. And the cigarettes of somebody else's dad.'

'Oh, Davie.'

And so I told him the banal old stuff and he blessed me and dismissed me.

When I went out, Maria was still waiting.

'Well,' she said. 'Do you feel holy and free now?'

I shook my head.

'I told him next to nowt.'

We walked up past the Half Way House and into Felling Square where we'd have to part.

She said, 'The way to say something is just to start saying the start of it, then everything will come out. Or you can just choose bits of it, and say them in any order. Or . . .'

She threw up her hands and laughed.

'And of course you don't have to say nowt at all.'

We looked around the square: the shadowy drinkers behind the frosted glass of The Blue Bell, people queueing to see *The Curse of Dracula* at the Corona, people climbing aboard the 82 to go to Newcastle. All so ordinary, all so tame.

'Or you could write it,' she said. 'Like a story. Then you could put the craziest things in and they wouldn't seem so crazy cos it'd just be a story.'

'I made a creature with Stephen Rose,' I muttered.

'Eh?'

'We made a man out of clay. We made him move, Maria. We made him walk. He came alive.'

I looked into her eyes.

'Do you believe me?' I said.

'Yes. It's crazy, but yes. What else?'

'Stephen Rose. He isn't a boy like . . .'

I couldn't go on.

'I'll tell you it bit by bit,' I said. 'It might take a long time.'

'OK,' she said.

Sergeant Fox and PC Ground drove past, stuffed into a little blue police car.

'Got to go,' I said.

We parted with a kiss. I ran uphill, and started to feel free at last. My sleep that night was dreamless and deep.

Next morning I looked out of my window. Dad was kneeling in the garden in the sunlight. Clay was stretched out on the earth beside him.

Fifty-Seven

Dad turned to me as I stepped out from the house. His eyes were wide with wonder.

'Davie, come and see!'

I shuffled across the grass.

'What is it, Dad?'

'Found it this morning in Braddock's Garden. All the blokes are getting stuff out – soil and plants and rocks – before they fill the quarry in.'

Clay's legs and an arm had fallen off and had been put back in place. A crevice had opened up between his head and shoulders. Clods of him had crumbled away.

'What do you think it is?' I said.

'God knows. Something ancient, I thought, then I saw it wasn't. He fell to bits when I put him into the barrow. I been putting him back together again.'

He was pockmarked by the rain. There were channels where the water had trickled over him. There were dried-out puddleholes in him. The whole bulk of him had slumped and softened. He was ungainly and twisted. Where he'd lain on the earth, he'd started to merge with it, turning back to the stuff called clay and not the creature Clay. But the sycamore seeds were still in him, and the hawthorn berries, and the ash keys. And he was so beautiful, and I looked at how he was now and I thought of how he had been, when he had walked beside me, when we had looked at each other in a window in the night and had seen each other standing together, so powerful and so lifelike and so strange. Dad reached down, and tried to smooth the clefts and cracks and creases. I touched, too, and I waited for Clay's voice inside me, but there was just silence.

'Must've been some kids, eh?' said Dad. 'Must've been some game or something.'

'Aye,' I said.

'Nowt to do with you and your mates?'

'No.'

'Or mebbe Stephen Rose?' he said.

'Dunno, Dad.'

'Anyway,' he said. 'A bit of clay'll come in useful in them sandy borders.'

'Not yet, though,' I said.

'No. He's too lovely right now. We'll wait till he's just a pile of muck. It'll be a while before I dig him in.'

Fifty-Eight

I brought Maria to him.

'He lived and walked,' I told her. 'I heard his voice inside my head.'

She gazed at him and said he was beautiful. She narrowed her eyes as she tried to see him as he was, a living thing instead of lifeless clay. Behind us Dad kept coming into and out of the garden, bringing heaps of soil, rocks and plants for a rockery, yelling how brilliant our garden would be.

'How did you do it?' asked Maria.

'It seemed so easy. It was just like this.'

I scooped a handful of clay out of Clay. I shaped it quickly to the shape of a man. 'Live,' I whispered. 'Move.' And of course nothing happened. I shrugged and laid the figure on the ground. I thought of Stephen, and wondered where he was now, what he was making now.

She picked up the figure. She walked it like a puppet on the grass. Then she squashed it into a ball.

'You couldn't have been wrong?' she said. 'Stephen couldn't have deceived you?'

I shook my head. I told her how Clay and I had walked alone together through the streets. How could that have been an illusion?

'Stephen was all lies and tricks,' I said. 'He told me lots of things that I don't believe. But there's some force in him, some power that the rest of us don't have.'

I said no more, but I knew that one day I'd have to say more, about devilry and madness and death.

'Do you think I'm mad?' I asked her.

She laughed.

'You? Mad?'

'Yes. What I've just told you – surely that's mad.'

'But isn't it the truth?'

'Yes. But sometimes I think I've caught something from Stephen. Sometimes I think I'm losing my mind.'

'You're not mad, Davie,' she told me.

She worked the ball of clay again. She made another figure from it and stood it on the grass.

'This is you,' she said. 'Sane and slightly barmy like all of us.' She took another piece of Clay and made another figure. 'And here is me, slightly barmy, too.'

So we went on making clay figures out of the body

of Clay, each one better and more lifelike than the one before. We named them as we worked: Geordie Craggs, Frances Malone, Crazy Mary, Prat Parker, Skinner and Poke, Father O'Mahoney, my mam and dad, Maria's mam and dad, and many more. Soon there was a little crowd before us.

Dad came up behind us, looked down and laughed.

'Haha!' he said. 'It's a congregation of the saints!'

Fifty-Nine

Clay's remnants still lie there in our garden. Dad can't bring himself to dig him in. Slowly, slowly, he is being washed into the sandy border, and earth returns to earth. The sycamore seeds and the hawthorn berries and ash keys have hatched and a little forest of saplings grows from him. Now the rose rises from his heart, the tiny conker tree seedling cracks open his skull. Time goes by. The seasons turn.

There's still no sign of Stephen Rose. Sometimes I think of him hiding out, practising his arts in Plessey Woods, or in Kielder Forest or the Cheviots, or in some distant empty wild place that has no name. I can't believe that he's gone for ever, that he won't return. I watch for reports of maiming and murder. A man is stabbed in North Shields. A girl is half-strangled in Whitley Bay. A teenager falls to his death on Marsden cliffs. There's no reference to Stephen Rose or a boy like Stephen Rose or to a monster, but I keep on watching, waiting, and at times I'm filled with dread.

Here in Felling, the memory of him is fading. There are whispers that he must be dead, of course, that he must have been abducted, that he'll be discovered in a shallow grave somewhere. When I find myself wishing that those things are true, I have to curb my thoughts.

Whatever happens, Crazy Mary still loves him and will always love him. A few weeks after Stephen went away, I walked through Felling to her door. It was a brilliant cloudless day. She took me in and made me tea and jam and bread. We sat on chairs at her back door and the sun poured down at us. She spoke so shyly, so sadly.

'The house is empty now,' she whispered.

I murmured something stupid about things getting better.

'The whole world is filled with nowt,' she said.

Her voice got even lower. Her hands trembled.

'I'm forgetting how to pray, son.'

I had the locket with me. I took it out and showed it to her.

'I didn't know what to do with this,' I said. 'I thought of you.'

I passed it to her. I showed her how to open it. She

fiddled at the catch with her scrawny fingers. She gasped as it clicked open.

'Oh, altar boy!' she said.

She dropped to her knees. She lifted them out, the stained cloth fragments, the dusty Sellotape. She held them up high. She closed her eyes and put the cloth and Sellotape on to her tongue and swallowed them. She clenched her hands tight and bobbed back and forward. Then opened her eyes, knelt up, and gazed into the sky.

'Oh, yes!' she said. 'Oh, look!'

I looked to where Crazy Mary looked.

'Look how Heaven has opened!' she said. 'Look how the angels come down to us!'

She tugged me to my knees.

'Do you see?' she gasped. 'Do you see them, son?'

I looked up at blue sky, at sunlight, at emptiness.

'Yes,' I told her. 'Yes, I do.'

She spread her arms wide.

'God is good!' she said. 'He will return! He will come home to us again.'

And ever since, her eyes have shone with hope.

This is the first time I've told the tale. I've tried to speak it, like Maria said – to speak it from the start and to keep on speaking it until everything is said, but each time I start, the craziness in it just brings me to a halt.

So now I've written it down, all of it. I don't care if there's craziness in it. I've learned that crazy things can be the truest things of all. You don't believe me? Doesn't matter. Tell yourself it's just a story, nothing more.